DISCIPLESHIP MATTERS

Learning from Timothy's Spiritual Journey

DR. MITCH MARTIN

Discipleship Matters: Learning from Timothy's Spiritual Journey

First Printing: 2015

ISBN 978-0-9885932-1-3

Edited by faithbasedediting.com, page design services by ChristianEditingServices.com, and book cover by equipcreative.com.

Printed in the United States of America.

Praise for Discipleship Matters

Mitch Martin has made the basics of discipleship and the essentials of Christian maturity an adventure in historical fiction. The book is clear and thoroughly biblical. It is an impressive and attractive way to present the basics of discipleship and to help us all better understand how our salvation impacts every aspect of our lives. This is a great tool for all and should be widely utilized in helping new converts grow in their faith ... and in helping older believers realize the treasure they have in Christ.

DR. JIMMY DRAPER - President Emeritus, LifeWay Christian Resources

The journey of Timothy's life and his relationship with Paul jumps off the pages of Discipleship Matters. Dr. Mitch Martin has unveiled the pinnacle importance of mentoring as we work to fulfill Christ's command to make disciples. This is a tool that can be used with new believers, mission teams, and leaders. The principles taught are the heartbeat of who Mitch Martin is in Christ.

STEVE BEST - Missions and Care Pastor, NorthStar Church

Dr. Mitch Martin has captured the biblical process of discipleship as seen in the relationship between Paul and Timothy. I gained new insight and was challenged by this compelling presentation of the discipleship process. Having the privilege of knowing Dr. Martin, I see how the Scriptures presented so beautifully in Discipleship Matters are lived out boldly and effectively in his life. I commend this book to every believer who has a desire to be a more faithful disciple.

DR. CHARLES FOWLER - Pastor, Germantown Baptist Church

While few would question the necessity of discipleship, far too few practice it with regularity and focus. Mitch Martin's book, Discipleship Matters presents both a compelling argument and a practical approach to discipleship that can be effectively woven into the lifestyle of any serious Christian. Mitch writes from conviction and experience, and this book will become a valuable tool that will shape your life.

DR. TOM ELLIFF – Former President, International Mission Board, SBC

Our church opened its doors for the first time in the fall of 2012. Discipleship Matters was used to show our men a picture of what true discipleship looks like. Combining biblical truth and historical fiction, this book proved to be exactly what was needed to launch our people into disciple-making.

DREW MURPHY - Pastor, Fayette Baptist Church

All parents treasure the moments when we see our children grasp spiritual realities as their own. In Discipleship Matters, Mitch Martin uses Christian fiction to show the importance of the mentor-mentee relationship of Christ-followers. Taught at our church as a discipleship course, these discoveries of the gospel framed in Timothy's life sparked a time of transformational learning in the heart of the youngest pupil— my twelve-year-old son, Harrison—as well some participants well into their seventies and eighties. I cannot overemphasize the value of presenting doctrine in this format!

DR. ASHLEY E. RAY - Pastor, Ridgeway Church

To my wonderful wife, Myra.
I love you.

"What you have heard from me in the presence of many witnesses entrust to faithful men who will be able to teach others also."

— 2 TIMOTHY 2:2 ESV

TABLE OF CONTENTS

Acknowledgements

If a book is the expression of what's in an author's mind and heart, then all who have made an impression on that writer deserve some of the credit when his book goes to print. In my case, first impressions began in a Christian home, so I'd like to say, "Thanks, Mom and Dad." Both in childhood and in the years since, countless preachers, writers, professors, friends, and intercessors have contributed to my life and helped to shape my faith and writing. Special thanks go to Steve Best, Henry Webb, Bob Holland, Kevin Ferrell, Kelly Seely, Richard Kuenzinger, Casey Pearson, Jon Kenney, Sarah Newman, Richard Miller, Ryan Sidhom, Jodi Skulley, and to the NET Bible for the maps included in the back. Deep appreciation goes to my son, Dustin; his wife, Candice; and to my daughter, Kristin, for their technical assistance and advice. Most of all, I am grateful for my wife, Myra, who has been patient and encouraging throughout the writing and revision marathon.

INTRODUCTION

Welcome to *Discipleship Matters: Learning from Timothy's Spiritual Journey*, a narrative Bible study based on the life of Paul's young protégé who became pastor to one of the most influential churches in the first century.

Timothy is the *only* New Testament character referred to as "a man of God."[i] His name is prominent throughout the New Testament. Of the twenty-seven books that comprise that part of the Bible, Timothy's name is found in twelve. The Apostle Paul considered Timothy "a beloved son"[ii] and referred to him as "a true son in the faith."[iii] Perhaps this is why Timothy is honored as a coauthor in six of Paul's thirteen epistles; and, although Paul most often wrote to congregations, he penned two personal letters directly to Timothy. Thus, Timothy is clearly linked to almost two-thirds of Paul's New Testament letters. Altogether his name is mentioned twenty-seven times in Scripture.

This remarkable individual received the gospel firsthand from the great missionary Paul. But to fully appreciate what that means, we must first grasp the gospel. Simply stated, it is the good news that God sent His Son Jesus to die as a substitutionary sacrifice for the sins of humanity and raised Him again to a new and victorious life so that all of His faith-followers may participate in His overcoming experience. I've chosen to highlight four gospel realities in this book:

1. The gospel involves both the death and resurrection of Jesus Christ. It's not just the death, but it's also the life of Jesus that saves.[iv]

2. The gospel facilitates identification between God and man. As the theologian John Quigley aptly put it, "God became as we are so we could become as He is." Through the gospel people become one with the Lord Jesus Christ.[v]

3. The gospel is experienced, initially and continuously, by repentance

and faith. The follower of Christ is called to a lifestyle of habitually turning away from sin and self while trusting in the Savior.

4. The gospel provides both justification and sanctification, meaning the gospel saves people from both the penalty of sin and the power of sin. Through the gospel the repentant believer is declared legally righteous and enjoys a right standing before God. This is called justification.[vi] Yet the gospel also enables the believer to experience daily victory over temptation. This divinely empowered righteous lifestyle is what is known as sanctification.[vii] Salvation is not only past tense, "I was saved," but present tense, "I am being saved."

We know Timothy initially received the gospel during Paul's first missionary journey. I've chosen to combine Scriptural insights with my own ideas to present Timothy's story as a narrative, and that means I have taken some license. I hope that when you've completed this book, you'll take time to learn more about Timothy both in the New Testament and through works such as *The New American Commentary* (Holman Reference), *Holman Bible Commentary* (Holman Reference), *The New Manners and Customs of the Bible* (Bridge-Logos), and *The Tyndale Concise Bible Commentary* (Tyndale House).

In *this* book Timothy, like many other new Christians, begins his journey to Christ with a mental commitment to the gospel that is in many ways shallow. As a result, Timothy continues to struggle deeply with insecurities and temptations. When Paul returns to Lystra on his second missionary journey, he finds Timothy full of limitless potential, yet languishing in spiritual infancy.

Two thousand years later, countless believers initially accept Christ into their lives, only to follow the same dismal trajectory. While these Christians may be authentically committed to Christ, they have no idea how to live out the gospel. They know they are saved, but yet—like young Timothy—they still struggle. And they may wonder what is wrong.

What they need is spiritual maturity. But maturity must be pursued. The solution is discipleship: Christ did not commission His followers to go and convert people to Christianity; He told us to make disciples.[viii] A disciple is one who learns and follows another, in the Christian's case, seeking to emulate and better serve Christ. Like Timothy, every Christian needs to be discipled. Every Christian must continuously learn and grow.

Yet in another sense, every Christian should also be like Paul, the great disciple-maker. The Christian life is a journey where every believer profits from encouragement and guidance. But we cannot just soak up these gifts; we must also seek to give them. As we follow Jesus—even if we are only getting started—we should reach back and pull others forward in their walks of faith.

Whether you consider yourself more like Timothy or like Paul based on my brief thoughts here, this book about discipleship will help nurture growth and understanding as you seek to follow Christ and help others along their spiritual journey.

In the chapters to come, please read the story as if it were Timothy's account of his experiences alongside Paul. At the end of each chapter, put yourself in Timothy's sandals by answering the "Grow as a Disciple" questions. Then think about your role as a disciple-maker, and answer the "Preparing to Disciple" questions. When you see the key icon, check out the related PowerPoint content. Maps are included in the back.

To get started, visit *mitchmartin.org/resources* and
watch the PowerPoint titled
"The Exchanged Life."

It will give you an outline of this book and
help you know what to expect.

PART ONE

From Paul, your brother in Christ.

To Timothy.

Greetings!

I long to see you so that I may be filled with joy, clearly recalling your sincere faith that first lived in your grandmother, Lois, then in your mother, Eunice, and that I am convinced is in you also.

— 2 TIMOTHY 1:4-5, author paraphrase

Chapter 1

DISCOVERING LOVE

A.D. 48

Those who knew him best started calling Paul "the man who won't stay dead" not long after his first missionary journey. The trouble began when Paul and Barnabas came to my hometown of Lystra and healed a crippled beggar. News spread quickly in our rural community within the Roman province of Galatia, and some of the townspeople tried to deify the evangelists, wrongly associating the pair with the Greek gods Zeus and Hermes. When Paul and Barnabas rejected their praise, it created an awful disturbance.[1] Before it was over, violent men from surrounding areas arrived;[2] they stoned Paul and dragged his body out of town—imagining the world was done with the preacher so vocal about the Christ.

But after the crowd dispersed, something remarkable happened. The local saints, followers of Jesus, encircled Paul's lifeless body. No sooner had they gathered than his spirit miraculously returned. How delighted they were when Paul got up and marched back into town with determination in his stride![3] In the years since, I've heard Paul testify of being caught up into the third heaven, into the splendor of paradise, where he heard unimaginable glories.[4] I've never asked him to confirm it, but I suspect the event happened the day he was stoned.

I, Timothy son of Achilles, was almost fifteen when Paul was beaten in Lystra, and I looked on him with awe when a friend brought him to our home that same day. As I listened to him speak of Jesus, I wondered: *What will I do with the words of this man who was beaten unconscious and yet wouldn't retreat? What might I learn from this preacher who refused to be silent? How can I ignore a martyr who won't stay dead? Surely*, I decided, *there must be something to this Christ he preaches.*

Before the sun went down that day, my mother and grandmother decided they liked Paul's words and adopted him as a friend. They invited Paul and Barnabas to stay in our home and to tell us more about his new religion.

Paul's message was unlike anything I'd ever heard before: he said the gods worshiped in our city were not gods at all, just stones. The true God, he said, is the same God long ago revealed through the Hebrew Scriptures so dear to my mother and grandmother. He created the whole world, and though He intended the world and all things in it to be "very good," humans chose to rebel against Him.[5] Our rebellion, our sin, separated the human race from Him. No matter how many sacrifices we offer, no matter how good we try to be, we can no longer enjoy relationship with our Creator. Only through God's loving plan could the gap separating us from Him be bridged. We desperately needed forgiveness and restoration, and the Lord determined to provide it.

To accomplish His plan, Paul explained, God came in human form. Jesus, God's Son, was born of a virgin and lived a life free of all sin. To show He was God in the flesh, Jesus calmed a storm, fed thousands with only a few loaves and fish, healed the sick, made the blind see, and even raised His friend Lazarus from the dead. But then He did the most important thing. He became the final sacrifice that could forever forgive our sins and provide a bridge of reconciliation between God and humans. He died on a cross. And rather than staying in the tomb where they laid Him, Jesus arose from the dead three days later. This,

Paul noted, shows that Jesus is not only the Messiah: He is the cure for death. Those who place their faith in Christ will not descend into Hades; they will spend eternity with the Lord.

Paul said two things were necessary if we were to receive the gift of salvation, that is, to inherit the promise of eternal life and restoration with God that can give us joy and peace during our lifetimes. First, we must repent of our sin. He said that means we need to turn away from, renounce, reject, and have nothing more to do with evil in any form. Second, he said we must believe in who Jesus is and in what He came to accomplish. According to Paul, we must put all of our confidence in Jesus and rely solely upon what He did when He died on the cross for our sins and rose again on the third day.

Following Paul's brief explanation, we divided into two groups. Barnabas remained seated on the floor with my mother and sister. Grandma and I went next door to her house with Paul.

Once inside Grandma's small house, Paul helped us put into words our desire to repent and believe in Jesus. Grandma prayed first; I prayed second. When I did, I told God I was sorry for my sin and asked Him to forgive me. I also told God I did believe in Jesus. I said I trusted the stories I'd heard about Him and had decided He was real—not just a myth, but truly the Son of God. I thanked Jesus for dying on the cross as a substitute for me; it was, after all, my sins He came to forgive. I thanked Him for rising again to give me new life. I asked Jesus to come into my life and take control.

When I finished praying, I lifted my head and looked around the room. Grandma beamed at me. Paul clapped a hand on my shoulder, joy evident in his eyes. While I didn't feel particularly different in that moment, I did feel a sense of relief. I would no longer have to worry about dying and falling to Hades.

We spoke for a while, Paul answering Grandma's many questions. When we arose, Paul shook my hand enthusiastically. He smiled and said something I would treasure for years to come. "I just *know* God's got special plans for your life, Timothy."

My heart felt light.

We headed outside where Barnabas and the others were waiting. Paul's parting instructions were three-fold: pray, read the Scriptures, and worship together every Sunday with the other local followers of Jesus. Together we would form the new church of Lystra.

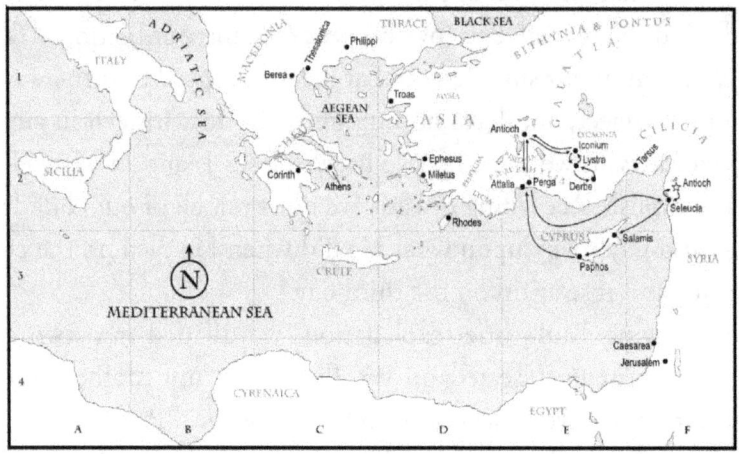

Unfortunately, in the twenty-four months that followed, I neglected to do what Paul suggested. I didn't pray, except when I was in trouble. I didn't read the Scriptures on a regular basis, though I could quote many thanks to Grandma's influence and my quick memory. And I only managed to gather with the other believers occasionally, often sitting in the back with my elbows on my knees and my head hung low. Consequently, my initial enthusiasm for Christ subsided. Over time I found myself battling the anger issues that had plagued me since the day my father deserted our family.

While I didn't know it then, I was what Paul called a *carnal* Christian. He believed there are only three types of people in the world: the natural, the spiritual, and the carnal. A natural man is someone who has never received Christ. He is dead to the things of God. A spiritual man is someone who has received Christ. She is alive to God and led by the indwelling Holy Spirit. But a carnal Christian, which is what I was early on, is someone who has received Christ but walks after his own fleshly desires rather than being led by the Spirit.[6] A carnal Christian is spiritually immature.

I quickly found that being a carnal Christian is no fun. In fact, it is downright miserable. I wanted people to think I was a sincere Christian like my mother, but I was out of fellowship with God. As a result, life felt like a battle. And I hate losing—even if only to myself in a private war.

Thankfully, Paul would soon return to Lystra, take me under his wing, and help me connect with Christ in a deeper way. The apostle helped me grow in my understanding and faith. In time, our interactions and the Holy Spirit's influence would ignite a flame in my heart. That fire, in fact, burns so brightly today that I've chosen to write an account of my struggle in hopes that it will help others grow closer to the Lord.

The long journey toward entrusting myself into the loving arms of Christ started in a bizarre way.

I had just limped home from a fight and stood in the backyard, trying to wash the blood—mine and Adam's—off my hand. While laboring over the self-inflicted wound, using an oak stump as my medical table, I caught a glimpse of movement behind me. I flinched. Mother always showed up at the worst times.

"What's that, Timothy?" she asked, peering over my shoulder. "Is that blood?"

My sixteen-year-old face grew hot, and I exhaled loudly. I did not want to tell the truth, to admit I had been fighting again. But I couldn't lie.

An awkward silence fell between us until Mother stepped beside me, her fleshy hand reaching out to grab my wrist. I jerked away from her, the basin of red water tipping onto the ground as I did. She gasped, stepping back quickly.

At first I hoped she would just go away, but the sound of her sniffling pulled at my heart. I frowned, turned, and looked Mother in the eye. "Please don't cry, Mother. The fight wasn't as bad as my hand looks. Besides, Adam had it coming."

"What happened? Not more teasing about your father?"

"Adam said Father left because of me," I said through clenched teeth, still so angry and hurt I thought I might forget how to breathe.

"So I punched him. And you know what? If he gives me any more grief, I'll hit him again."

Mother was quiet for a moment, clearly trying to decide what to say. I had known Adam all my life. He was a couple of years older than me and often tormented smaller kids. But he wasn't as tough as he wanted everyone to think, and I wasn't about to let him bully me without retaliating. My Uncle Joe, a boxer in his younger years, showed me the difference between a left jab and a right hook. He said I could use a combination of the two to silence Adam when he bothered me. Just as expected, I found that the left jab didn't do much damage, but the follow-up, vicious right hook I'd delivered sent Adam reeling.

"Adam is over a head taller than you, Timothy. He could have hurt you." Mother stepped closer.

I lifted my chin. "He could have tried."

"You can't go around hitting people. That's not the way of our Lord," she said.

I retorted, "Uncle Joe doesn't have a problem with fighting, and he is a believer too."

Mother sighed, gently pushing my hair back from my forehead as she'd done when I was small and life was simple. "Oh, Timothy. I've told you before. your father didn't leave us because of you. He was unhappy with me, Son. If anyone is to blame, it's me. Not you."

I felt sick to my stomach and wanted the conversation to be over. Thankfully, Mother ended it for me. "You need to quit worrying about Adam and start focusing on your chores," she said. "A messenger came today. He said the apostle Paul should be arriving sometime this week. I know how you like to trail him, but that field must be plowed before I can afford to have all your attention directed elsewhere. Now finish cleaning up and get inside. Supper will be on the table soon."

Every day over the next week, I arose at first light, working to complete my chores in record time. Chief on my list of duties was plowing; up and down our gentle rolling hillsides I marched. By Friday my mood was much improved; springtime always had a positive effect on me. Daffodils poked their yellow heads up, and robins pulled worms from the earth as the bright sunshine worked to dispel the cold. A bit of snow still lay alongside the northern edges of the buildings, but I knew it would melt soon.

I was about to head toward the well for a long drink when I spotted a small crowd approaching the edge of town. On a brisk, sunny morning in Lystra, it feels as though you can see forever. I smiled when I realized the group was headed toward the well too. I recognized most of them as fellow Christ-followers, or people of the Way. In the heart of the group stood our friend Paul, who brought a stranger into our midst.

I soon learned the stranger's name was Silas; he was a big man who didn't say much. Silas looked like a gladiator with a thick black beard, round chest, and massive arms. He could not have looked less like bent, scholarly Paul.

Paul and Silas taught among the people over the coming days. I never missed a church gathering in that time, and I found myself just as drawn to the Scriptures when Paul taught them as I had been during our first encounter. After a few weeks passed and several dozen more townspeople became believers, Paul pulled me aside. He told me the Lord had something special planned for me. He insisted I was destined for greatness.

"How would you like to come along with me and Silas?" Paul asked, his smile lighting his eyes.

"Come along?" I asked, feeling a shiver of excitement. Travel with Paul? Could a young farmer ever expect a better opportunity? "Where? What would I need to do?"

"We'll go where the Lord sends us, Timothy. We serve as frontline ambassadors for King Jesus, who is, as you know, coming soon to finish setting up His kingdom here on earth." He drew in a deep breath, smiled up at the sky, and exhaled slowly. "I suspect you would be an excellent missionary. Lord willing, you may even pastor one of the churches one day."

"Me?"

"Why not you, Son?"

I thought about my fighting, my anger, and my failure to follow through on the three things Paul had asked me to do in his absence. But then my mind caught on what Paul—Paul the great apostle—had called me. He called me *Son*. I couldn't remember my own father ever calling me that.

"I'd love to join you, Mr. Paul," I replied, looking down at my feet, suddenly self-conscious.

He placed a hand on each of my forearms. "Now, none of that. You don't have to call me mister. Just call me Paul. And know I will be pleased to have you accompany us in this important work."

I nearly whooped with delight before thinking better of it. Instead, I stood up straight and said something about needing my mother's approval before I accepted. My leaving would remove male presence from her home, quite possibly forever since travel was risky and the times were not particularly kind to the followers of Jesus.

"Of course, you must ask," Paul agreed. "But Silas and I both believe you could be a powerful asset to our team. We've noticed two qualities that give you exceptional potential for missionary service. You know the Scriptures[7] and you are likable.[8] I've rarely seen a boy so quick to memorize Torah, the Prophets, and our Lord's words. You do in a day what some can do only over months."

I smiled, genuinely pleased by the praise.

"Think it over," Paul said as he turned to meet up with Silas at a village not far from town. "We have to go back to Derbe to check on the church there. We should be back in seven to ten days, no more than two weeks. Hopefully when we return, you will be ready to give us a positive answer."

That afternoon I quickly gained Mother's approval and Grandma's too, but the task before me made me increasingly ashamed of the fact that I'd happily lived as a baby Christian for the two years since Paul first introduced me to the Lord. Mother, knowing me better than anyone, seemed to read my uneasiness. She commented that some birds never find their wings unless they are first pushed from the nest. I knew what she meant: she felt my struggles were tied to my anger in growing up in a home without a father. Perhaps in being forced away from the scene of my struggle I just might find freedom from the old habits that haunted my thoughts and soured my actions.

When it came down to it, I simply wanted to be happy. I knew my emotions went up and down too often and that I completely missed out on the abundant life Paul said Christ's followers could enjoy. But I wasn't entirely certain happiness was something I could ever find—it certainly wasn't in Lystra. Would I find it on the road with Paul? Would I grasp happiness as I investigated the big cities and as I encountered the kind of adventures that seemed to find Paul? I could not be sure of the answers, but I suspected this invitation to travel with him might be exactly what I'd been looking for.

Early that evening in our one-room home, my older sister Hitty gave her unsolicited opinion on my plans while Mother was out visiting with a neighbor. She'd overheard Mother's enthusiasm when I'd brought up the subject of traveling with the great evangelist, and her tight lips and flared nostrils made it clear how she felt about the whole thing. Hitty, like me, struggled with anger. "Do you have any brains under those curly locks of yours?" she demanded as she put away the dinner dishes. "You're still a child. You don't know the first thing about missionary service."

I clenched my fists, having expected nothing less than this kind of scolding from Hitty. "I'm seventeen years old, Hitty. I think I can figure it out."

She pointed her finger at my chest, her usually fair skin glowing red. "You are *not* seventeen. You're only *sixteen!*"

"I turn seventeen in less than two months."

"As if that matters," Hitty huffed. "Missionary life is too tough for you, Brother. You'll get homesick and be back in less than a week."

I could feel heat warm my neck as I raised my fist in a threatening gesture.

Hitty looked at the fist and slammed the clay vessel she was holding down onto the wooden table, knowing I wouldn't strike her but just as certain that I wanted to. She opened her mouth to insult me again when Mother stepped into the room.

"Timothy is old enough to decide what he wants to do with his life," Mother soothed. "We will miss him, but the Lord will take care of us and will give him courage."

Hitty sighed as if exasperated with both of us and stomped out of the house while Mother went to work at her loom.

The same day Paul and Silas left for Derbe, Nicolas DoM showed up in Lystra. Nicolas preferred people call him DoM, short for "Defender of Moses." To me the nickname had always sounded pretentious, as I didn't think the great Hebrew lawgiver Moses needed defending. But Nicolas said Moses was the greatest prophet ever and should be respected as such—particularly in "days like ours," whatever that meant.

For the last couple years Nicolas had regularly invaded our little town like a military hero, accompanied by a parade of fifteen or twenty long-bearded Pharisees who marched behind him or clustered around him wherever he went. This particular occasion proved no exception. Even when the group gathered for what looked like no other purpose than getting out of the sun, they were all dressed expensively and in full religious regalia. Across their foreheads were *phylacteries*, small boxes of Scripture strapped above their eyes. At their feet, tassels grazed the dusty courtyard. Their finery seemed to mock the simple clothing and ways of most of the local people.

Several days after his arrival, a few of us passed near the group's shade tree when Nicolas called out to us, clearly hoping to draw listeners. He loudly explained that he and his team had come to Lystra to strengthen the Christians among us. "As you know," he boasted in a tone that demanded notice and anticipated respect, "I've studied the Torah extensively. I know its great importance. One cannot follow Jesus Christ unless one follows Moses. Come, learn from me."

Nicolas was known for his religious rants, but these words were a bold thing to say. Less than two years ago Paul had nearly lost his life for the name of Jesus in my town. I paused, though my companions scurried on to their work. Clearly Nicolas DoM and the others meant to learn more about the growing church in Lystra. I suddenly found myself wondering why.

As I approached the group, I thought about what I knew of Nicolas DoM from Antioch. Rumor had it the man had suffered through a rough upbringing, his mother turning to prostitution much as the prophet Hosea's wife had done. His father, people claimed, compensated for the embarrassing event by staying out at sea for most of his son's boyhood. Nicolas, in response to the shame and abandonment, swore he'd be a better person. Indeed, he became highly religious, even to the point of growing fanatical—though he changed religions often in his quest to find what best suited him. Multiple dramatic conversions led him to switch from paganism to Judaism and then to Christianity. It was after that final switch that the Jerusalem church elected Nicolas as one of the original seven deacons.[9] But Paul had warned our little church to beware of anyone—teacher, angel, or deacon—who insisted the old sacrificial laws so important under Moses must be zealously followed by all who come to Christ. More and more, it seemed, Nicolas DoM gave cause for other professing Christians to be wary. I'd overheard speculation that his own conversion might be more of an act than reality.

"I'd like to speak with you, Nicolas DoM," I said, grateful no one had stopped to hear the pompous speech he hoped to make. "Privately."

He raised an eyebrow, said something to the Pharisee at his right, and rose. "Of course, young Timothy," he boomed. "This way."

I headed in the direction he'd indicated by the tilt of his head, and the two of us were soon well away from his group of followers.

"And how are you, old friend?" Nicolas asked, clearly sizing me up and likely noticing I'd grown taller and heavier since his last visit to our small town. "How is planting?"

"I'm well," I answered. "We are still working part of Uncle Joe's farm. The wheat has been sown, and it should be a good year for our hazelnuts, figs, and apricots. Mother suggested we grow tea this year; that should do well."

He seemed to mull over my words before squinting into my eyes, clearly calculating. "And you are interested only in the harvesting of produce these days?" His hand smoothed his beard into a point as he watched me.

I knew what he was really asking. Was I involved in working the Lord's fields, helping to bring souls into the kingdom of God? I stood to my full height. "If you've heard rumors that I'm joining Paul on his next journey, you heard right. I do plan to join the Lord's laborers."

Just as I suspected, Nicolas's face darkened at the mere mention of Paul's name. Paul taught that salvation comes by God's grace through faith in Jesus. Nicolas was increasingly vocal in his theory that rule-keeping was just as important as trusting in Christ. "You should reconsider, boy." *Was that a threat I heard in his oily voice?* "Paul is unstable. He violates the laws of Moses and encourages others to do the same. You can't separate Christianity from Judaism any more than you can remove a tree from its trunk. One grows out of the other, just as sure as night follows day."

I frowned. That didn't sound right to me, but I couldn't quite refute him.

"Why, I doubt you've even been circumcised," he thought aloud, "your father being a Greek. Surely you know better than to play the missionary when you haven't first submitted to the sign of the covenant."

My face warmed, embarrassment warring with defensiveness. "Well, I'm going. I like Paul."

Nicolas changed tactics, his voice soothing. "I just don't want you to get hurt, Timothy. As the Psalmist says, 'Don't walk with the wicked or stand with the sinner.'[10] That's why we must avoid troublemakers like Paul."

I wondered what Moses would say about Nicolas DoM casting doubt on Paul's character. "Paul's *not* evil," I retorted.

Nicolas clearly did not like the force of my words. He took a half step forward, now standing only inches from my face. "He *is* wicked," he hissed, then softened his voice. "You just don't know it yet."

Nothing within me believed him, but everything within me was suddenly sure that "deacon" Nicolas DoM was no friend of the church and was certainly no friend to me. A wave of anger clouded my vision and before I could think better of it, I charged forward and smacked my forehead against Nicolas's hooked nose.

He yelped and stumbled backward, blood pouring from his nostrils. "Why you little half-breed![11] You did that on purpose!"

"I'm sorry," I lied.

With one hand he tried to stop the blood running over his lips and with his other he pointed a finger at me. "You," he said, "are rabble. Christ will have nothing to do with the likes of you!"

I flinched in spite of myself.

"Mark my words," he said menacingly, just before he stomped back to his group, "If you dare to join up with Paul, I will personally cut your throat in the middle of the night, while you are sleeping."

I blanched, surprised by this shocking glimpse of the villain behind the religious mask. It occurred to me as I thought about his wide, angry jaw and beady, narrow eyes that he looked like a snake. Never again would I be fooled by his forked tongue. "I doubt Paul and the others will like knowing that you threatened murder," I called to his retreating back. "I seem to recall that conflicts with one of Moses' commands."

He turned to me with malice in his eyes, motioning me to be silent. "If you ever say a word of this to anyone," he promised, "I'll kill your mother … right after I take care of you."

Nicolas and his showy crew disappeared soon after our confrontation. His threats only made me more determined to go with Paul, but the look in his eyes continued to bother me. That night, after I'd fed the ox, I went to see Grandma. Her one-room home was next to ours. While I had no intention of telling her about my conversation, I found myself giving her the gist of it anyway. Though she seemed saddened by what I shared, she did not seem surprised.

Grandma sighed. "It is just as Paul warned in his letter to the churches here in Galatia. He said, 'Guard your freedom. Watch out for legalists. Don't go back to slavery.'[12] That Nicolas and his bunch are rule followers, not Jesus followers. How wrong he is to threaten a young man determined to follow Christ."

"But what if he wasn't just making empty threats?" I asked. "I don't care so much about me, but I want you and Mother to be safe."

She chuckled, probably because she thought I'd exaggerated my encounter. "Oh, Eunice and I will be fine. Don't worry about us. God has never let us down, and He'll take care of us till the day we fall asleep in the Lord or He comes back."

Her assurance calmed me.

"This is a marvelous, once-in-a-lifetime opportunity," she said as we sat in front of her small fire. "I wish I was younger, and I'd go with Paul too! Forget about Nicolas. Go share your faith with others. I want you to. I insist."

We clasped hands and she squeezed my calloused palms. "Now," she said, "I want to give you something." Her eyes were deep pools of love and knowledge under silvery-white brows. She looked so old and wise that I knew whatever she would give me would be special. "Timmy, have you ever heard of the Royal Prayer?"

I thought for a moment. "No, I don't think so. Why do they call it royal?"

"It is called the Royal Prayer," she answered, "because it was prayed by King David to the Lord. It goes like this: 'When I am afraid, I put my trust in you.'[13] Say it with me."

I repeated it with her three times, though I had it as soon as the sentence was out of her mouth.

"When you are on your missionary trip, you can pray that prayer whenever you have a need. And you can change the words to fit your situation. For example, you can pray: 'When I am angry, I will trust in You. When I am sad, I will trust in You. When I am lonely, I will trust in You.'"

I nodded.

"The Royal Prayer is the prayer of kings, and it has helped me hundreds of times," she concluded. "It will help you too, my sweet boy."

Three days later I accepted Paul's invitation, trusting God would take care of me in spite of Nicolas's threats and my own shortcomings.

The church leaders ordained me for the gospel ministry[14] and designated me as an evangelist.[15] Though I had much to learn, I was enthusiastic about our mission.

To celebrate my ordination, the church gave me a new sheepskin shoulder bag. Its white woolen strap felt fluffy and comfortable against my neck. It added a swagger to my steps and made me feel like quite the adventurer when the other young people in our group peppered me with questions just before we headed out. My excitement was so high that I felt a new bounce in my step, and I could hear my voice getting stronger and deeper. *Already I'm happier than I've been in years,* I told myself, expecting the next few months to grow better and better.

"Yes," I answered my friend Zachariah, "we will visit some big cities, maybe Ephesus or Byzantium."[16]

"When will we come back?" I repeated Hannah's question. "I'm not sure."

"Won't I miss my mother's cooking, Atreus asks!" I laughed. "Of course I will miss her food. No one cooks better than she does."

Would I kill any more wolves? Peter wanted to know. I thought about that, remembering the big black wolf I'd downed last winter. Unbidden, a picture of dangerous Nicolas DoM came to mind. "Only if we are threatened," I promised.

Moments later, I hugged all my family members—even Uncle Joe, who promised to take care of Mother in my stead. After that I stepped out on the rocky road north of town and fell in step behind Paul and Silas. I was on my way!

My companions laughed at my enthusiasm. Spring was in the air, and a spring was in my step. On the outskirts of town, as if to mimic my joy, a calf in my friend Jacob's pasture kicked up his heels while a line of geese honked as they flew overhead. In fact, everything was perfect until a rock sailed past my ear, narrowly missing my skull.

Paul and Silas immediately tensed at the commotion. "Who is that?" Silas asked, scanning the hillside to our right where a young man about my age stood, smirking down at me.

"That's Adam," I answered, thinking it was pretty low of him to attack me when I wouldn't see it coming. "Just a friend telling me good-bye."

"And apparently good riddance too," Silas added, sending Adam a disapproving scowl.

We traveled north from Lystra, going from village to village. At each stop Paul would find the Christian converts from his first missionary trip. At any stops that didn't have any converts, he'd go the synagogue if there was one. After that, he would join us out in the community as we told people about Jesus. In nearly every village, new faces joined the family of Christ and were funneled into new or existing churches. Most of the young believers received their newfound faith with joy, but some were negative and whiny. Paul said not to let their attitudes bother me. "We share the good news," he said. "But ultimately all believers have to decide for themselves whether they want to rejoice in the Lord or not."

About ten days into our journey, in the misty predawn hours, I awoke to the sound of voices. As I opened my eyes, I was surprised to see four men rummaging through our campsite. Panic surged through my heart. *Are Nicolas and his men making good on his threats?* In less than a second, I was wide-awake. I jumped up and looked around.

Each of the men, clearly bandits, held large knives. While we had relatively few supplies, they were taking most of them. One even clutched my new sheepskin bag, which had been tied to my bedding and was now cut free.

I foolishly marched across the campsite to reclaim my bag, but one of the men swung his knife at me. At Paul's insistence, I backed off and allowed the lowlifes to slither away. The only thing I didn't lose in the robbery was a tiny leather sack of coins I had hidden in a bush the night before.

Each of us frustrated, Paul, Silas, and I soon broke camp without a word. Silas gave me an outer garment to wear. I thanked him, cinched up the oversized garment with a borrowed sash that drug the ground as I walked, and tied up my bedroll. The fog retreated as the sun rose, and Paul said, "Let's go. We're burning daylight."

We trudged along in silence for several miles. I paid no attention to the waterfalls or the meadows full of mountain flowers, my eyes pointed downward. I was deep in thought. *Should I continue on the journey without any gear, clothes, or belongings? Or should I go home and work until I can resupply all I've lost?* The thought of taking the latter option and hearing Hitty tell me, "I told you so," convinced me I was better off to keep moving forward without supplies.

"Don't you worry, Timothy," Paul encouraged me. "The Lord will provide for us. We'll see you have a new garment when we reach the next city."

I smiled in reply, but I wondered. *Is the theft a sign we do not have God's favor? Is it possible God doesn't love me as much as Paul and Silas—whose bags were not stolen?*

When we made camp that evening, I kept quiet. I felt angry, confused, perturbed—all the things that had discouraged me from living out the Christian life in the months following my acceptance of Jesus. After dinner, I sat on a log, crossed my arms, and stared at the campfire.

The men left me to my thoughts until Silas finally fell asleep. At that point, Paul joined me. "Look here," he whispered as he reached for a stick in our small woodpile. Then, in the orange glow of the campfire, Paul drew a circle in the dirt between us. Then he drew another circle about twelve inches beneath it.

"What is that?" I asked.

"This top circle represents Christ," he whispered warmly, "and this lower circle represents you."

He looked at me until I nodded that I understood. Then Paul drew a heavy line from one circle to the next, clearly making a solid connection between the two distant points. "Christ came down to this earth and died for *you*, Timothy," Paul said.

"I know that," I said.

"But do you know why?"

"Of course," I said. "He did it because He loves me. He loves all of us."

"Correct," he said with a smile in his whisper. "You were bought with the precious blood of Jesus."[17] He paused, shifted on the log under us. "Now, you know God adores His Son, Jesus, and yet He gave Him up for *you*. Is it not obvious, then, how very much God the Father and Jesus the Son cherish you?"

"You're right," I nodded, realizing that Paul had been mentally plotting this lesson for me all day. "I shouldn't allow the robbery to make me question whether I am loved."

He nudged my shoulder with his own. "Today was hard," he said, "and there are times when I need a reminder too."

I liked his transparency, but I knew I was not the Christ-follower he was. I blurted, "But what if we were robbed this morning because I've messed up? Because I'm not good enough? Because I still struggle with sin?"

Paul shook his head, "Don't think that way, Son. It stems from the kind of legalism Nicolas and his followers spread. Even if you were doing a horrible job—and you are not—God would still love you. The Lord does not love you more when you obey or less when you disobey. We know this is true because when we were undeserving sinners, God loved us and sent His Son.[18] We do our best, but we must trust in His grace. His love is unconditional."

I felt tension ease from my shoulders as Paul put an arm around me. "Whether you obey or disobey, live or die, or if angels or demons encircle you, nothing in this world—past, present, or future—will ever affect God's love for you.[19] As God said through the prophet Isaiah, 'My steadfast love shall not depart from you.'[20] You believe the words of Isaiah, don't you, Timothy?"

"Yes, sir, I do. But what about my father, Paul? Does God's love really extend to men who leave their families? To a man who walks out on the kindest woman on earth and abandons his own children?"

"God said through the prophet Jeremiah, 'I have loved you with an everlasting love,'"[21] he replied. "Since God's love is eternal, we know His love never wavers. And since God's love never changes, we also understand that an individual cannot cause His love to increase or decrease. And since God's love is constant, we know His love is *always* unconditional and unmerited."

Paul stood up and dusted himself off. "So, young Timothy, God loves all of us. You. Me. Your father. Even those men who stole our supplies. Tonight you have a choice. You can pout and be angry ... or you can focus your thoughts on Jesus. The ability to rejoice requires the proper choice. You must direct your thoughts toward Christ." He raised his voice above a whisper. "You are the only one who can do that."

I watched Paul stoke the fire until the coals were bright red. Then he put another log on the pile and unrolled his blanket.

When I laid my head down later, angry thoughts still tormented me. I remembered the ungrateful new Christians and the four bandits stealing my gear. In my mind I saw Adam hurling rocks at us and remembered my father's retreating back. Each of these irritants infuriated me. But thankfully I also remembered Paul's words, and I decided to try them. Rather than yielding to my anger, I spent the next moments training my mind upon the goodness of Jesus and the love of God.[22]

In the solemn silence of the night, an owl hooted. The stars above shone bright in the cold mountain air. A shooting star streaked across the sky. I closed my eyes, rolled over on my side, and pulled the blanket up tight. I thanked God for His love. And as I dozed off, I felt wrapped in something better than happiness and warmer than wool: I felt thoroughly loved and accepted in spite of myself.

Will this last? I wondered sleepily. Only time would tell.

Grow as a Disciple:

In this fictionalized account, Timothy felt abandoned by his father, essentially unloved. Summarize the lesson Paul taught Timothy with regard to this topic of love.

Which of the following words describe God's love? Circle all that apply.

sacrificial, unconditional, finite
immeasurable, temporary, eternal
fickle, undeserved, earned

"The ability to rejoice requires the proper choice." How can you train your brain to rejoice rather than to dwell on negative topics?

Memory Verse:

Commit to memory either John 15:13 or Romans 5:8. Write it here for practice. _____
_____
_____
_____

Prepare to Disciple Others:

Based on what you've read in this chapter, how might you encourage someone who has been victimized like Timothy? _____
_____
_____
_____
_____

Chapter 2

DISCOVERING CHRIST'S GUIDANCE

I woke up rested and refreshed. The world looked brighter, better. Paul's words about the extent of Christ's love for me had healed something deep inside me. The change was not staggering but subtle. It renewed my enthusiasm for our journey—at least momentarily—and it set me to thinking about the happier adventures that surely lie ahead.

"Silas," I asked, as we broke camp, "have you ever been to the big city of Ephesus?"

"No," he said, in his typically curt way, "but I've seen Jerusalem and Syrian Antioch."

I was just about to ask him about what he'd experienced in Jerusalem when Paul stopped in the road ahead of us and rubbed his eyes. He'd been doing that a lot throughout our trip.

Paul sighed, blinking hard in the sunshine. "I need to find an herbalist." He winced. "Soon. Just as soon as we reach the next city."

"Why? What's wrong?" I asked. In those days few were quick to rush to a doctor.

"My left eye is blurry," he answered, moving further down the path;

Paul was always eager to cover as much ground as we could on travel days. "Thank the Lord my right one sees clearly."

"It's gotten worse over the last several months," Silas noted. "A physician should examine you."

A day later we entered Pisidian Antioch, an ancient crossroads town nestled in the mountains. There Paul reunited with a physician named Luke who fussed over the apostle for a full week. (Like me, Luke was two years old in the Lord, having been converted during Paul's first missionary journey.) After a long prayer in which our little group asked for guidance and wisdom, Luke meticulously tried every conceivable remedy to alleviate Paul's blurry vision. Regrettably, despite painful experimentation, Luke could not improve Paul's eyesight. He did, however, encourage Paul's heart, eventually agreeing to accompany us on the next leg of our journey as Paul's personal traveling physician and a missionary wholly dedicated to Christ.

In the days leading up to our departure, I had excitedly anticipated our band of four heading toward glamorous Ephesus, but rather than turning west toward the grand city, we continued north. This did not fit well with my personal plans, and I already was feeling frustrated because the Lord had chosen not to heal Paul's eyes. So when Paul turned ahead of us in the general direction of Byzantium, I kicked a rock down the trail and muttered my disappointment, thinking no one would notice. Byzantium was no Ephesus.

Not far into our journey we traveled across a high plateau until we came to the edge of a bluff surrounded by pine trees. Just ahead of Luke and Silas, Paul bounded up a hill, put one foot up on a boulder and scanned the rugged region below. I noticed he squeezed his problem eye shut as he did so. Then he pointed out over the valley and made a wide sweeping gesture with his other hand. "One day 'the earth will be filled with the knowledge of the glory of the Lord as the waters cover the sea,'" he quoted from the writings of Habakkuk.[23] Then he paused, smiling widely. "We can never forget that, friends." He scrambled back down to us, surprisingly nimble on the steep embankment, and smiled. "Never forget."

We continued onward, and I mentally applauded our leader for his steadfast focus. Though Paul hadn't met Christ during His earthly lifetime, Paul loved Him and acknowledged Him in everything he did. Rather than growing discouraged by his ailment, he was choosing to trust in the Lord's plans for him—even though that plan apparently included letting him slowly lose his vision. Yes, the man with the brown, bald head; black mustache; neat beard; and bowed legs had chosen to center his life on the Lord, and he remained faithful.

Generally, Paul was an excellent leader, and I admired his decisiveness as we passed through lands unfamiliar to me. He possessed a keen sense of direction and remained in constant forward motion. But during those days in the region of Phyrgia and Galatia, Paul began to seem irritated, bewildered. Rather than maintain the constant course we had come to expect, he began to change directions many times. Sometimes we'd even backtrack. It was as if Paul was suddenly unsure of himself. And that aimlessness coupled with the growing, uncharacteristic scowl on his face slowly began to shake my confidence in him.

One morning I'd made up my mind to respectfully ask Paul why we seemed to be traveling in circles and switchbacks, quickening my pace to pass Silas and Luke so I could speak to our leader in private. But just as I approached him, Paul stopped in the middle of the path and focused on something up ahead. I looked to see what had caught his attention and paled at the sight of an approaching procession. Nicolas DoM and his little band of long-bearded Pharisees would soon be upon us.

I remembered Nicolas's threats and widened my stance, lowering my chin and preparing to glare in my enemy's eyes as soon as he got close enough to notice. But Paul, having heard all about Nicolas's words to me by that time, told me to be at peace and marched forward as if to keep distance between the foe and me.

The pompous group neared, and in spite of the cool mountain air, their conversation with our leader proved to be heated. Luke, Silas, and I couldn't hear every word said between the apostle and the dangerous deacon, but we could not miss Paul's insistence that Nicolas's group not try to follow us. He quoted several pieces of his letter to the churches at Galatia before finally concluding, "The gospel does not *need* the law of Moses added to it. If you are so concerned about circumcision, go cut yourselves!"[24] Apparently his insistence and volume were enough to make both the Pharisees and their leader turn in the path and retreat as fast as they could, tassels flapping wildly. Nicolas DoM didn't even look in my direction once—much to my relief. Paul stood with his hands on his hips, watching them retreat until they disappeared from sight.

That afternoon as we walked, Paul spoke candidly. He did not tell us exactly what had transpired in his meeting along the path, but he did say that much of our missionary work could be lost should the Defenders of Moses continue to preach their departures from truth. The agitators essentially wanted to turn people away from Jesus in favor of a return to old-fashioned legalism, teaching that God could be pleased not simply by a person's acceptance of Christ but also by his working to secure and maintain salvation through rule-keeping and tradition.

"Sounds like the real trouble," Luke summarized, "is that the Pharisees assisting Nicolas are impressive in appearance and logic. They argue the nuances of Scripture, separate themselves from 'sinners,' and seemingly apply God's Word to all aspects of their lives. They look as if they have it all together."

Paul nodded. "Quite the show they put on, isn't it?" He sighed. "Their religious debating skills make them superb recruiters of new converts, but they preach a gospel other than the one our Lord prescribed.[25] This source of contention between us, then, is a battle between freedom and slavery. We are struggling to liberate the souls of men and women while Nicolas and his men use religious hypocrisy to promote a pious form of bondage. But you and I know it is for freedom that Christ has set us free."[26]

The thought of Nicolas enslaving others through his deceit sickened me, and it made me realize I'd allowed myself to be enslaved by him too. I had lived in fear of his threats on my life and on my family for weeks. *No more,* I told myself. *I won't let that windbag haunt my thoughts any longer.*

The next day as we chopped our way through thick underbrush, we heard what sounded like a rushing roar up ahead. "Rapids," Silas noted as we approached the edge of a once dry wadi now swollen with white, churning water.

We nodded, scanning the shore for a narrow crossing point. Luke and Paul finally led the way to a place several yards upstream that was only a few feet in width, shouting their idea to use ropes and logs to build a temporary bridge from one side of the torrent to the other.

For a few minutes we worked toward this plan until Paul lowered the end of the log he and Silas carried and said loudly, "It's no good. This is too much work to get us across that space before nightfall. I think we can wade it."

We approached the stream arm in arm, wading across it one after the next as if we were an inseparable human chain. Down into the icy water we went: Paul, Luke, me, and then Silas. We held on to each other for stability as the water rushed first around our ankles, then knees, and then briefly up to our chests as we neared the center. The river rocks were slippery, and I had just thought how easily one of us could lose his footing when Silas did just that. Without making a sound, he disappeared under the water and released his hold on my hand. Horrified, I watched huge Silas swirl downstream, his head bobbing in the water as the current carried him away.

The next moments seemed to unfold in slow motion. Paul and Luke scrambled onto the bank, but I didn't follow them. Instead, I gave myself over to the stream's power, hoping it would take me right to Silas. He was advancing so quickly that I feared he would soon disappear from sight. Thankfully, the water did carry me to Silas, and my heart was pounding from the wild ride when I reached him. Together we landed against a fallen tree lying half in the water and half safely on shore. Both exhausted, we helped one another use the tree as a ladder out of the stream.

We sloshed and staggered up the steep bank. Our clothes clung to us, making us clumsy. We were both cold and winded. But we were alive, and that seemed no small miracle. I bent double, hands on my knees, and worked to catch my breath once we'd reached level ground. Luke and Paul ran toward us. As they neared, Silas shook his head back and forth to clear his thick black hair out of his eyes. He looked so much like a beast shaking itself dry after a swim that I started to laugh. Almost immediately, usually stoic Silas began to chuckle too.

The next day as we hiked, I lagged back to talk to Silas. Paul always led the way when we traveled, often accompanied by Luke—who seemed to ask endless questions, particularly about the life of Christ—and Silas usually brought up the rear. As it seemed Silas and I had reached a new level of friendship back at the stream crossing, I decided to take my concerns to him rather than Paul as I'd planned.

"Silas, I don't want to complain, but this nonstop wandering is starting to bug me."

"Wandering?" he asked, as if it had never occurred to him that our travel path was anything less than direct. "What do you mean?"

I laughed. "You know? The way we keep zigzagging back and forth like swallows in a feeding frenzy? We went west, then north, then east, and then back to the west. But no matter which way we go, sooner or later, Paul shakes his head and complains. 'No, no. This is not right!'"

Silas looked at me oddly and said, "We follow Paul as he follows Christ."

"I know that," I said cheerfully. "I just wonder why lately it seems Paul can't make up his mind."[27]

"I'm sure Paul knows what he is doing," Silas said.

I should have taken his response as the end of the matter. Unfortunately, there was more I wanted to say. "I joined this team in hopes of seeing some big cities, Silas." He didn't look at me, so I continued, "We didn't even get to see the temple of Artemis: everybody knows that's one of the greatest wonders in the world. If we keep going northwest, we won't get to see Byzantium either. All we do is walk and change course. Walk and change course. Aren't we ever going to stop and see something?"

Silas was quiet for a long moment, leaving me to feel uncomfortably aware that I was complaining against my leader just as the wandering Israelites had spoken against their leader Moses. The realization shamed me. Finally Silas broke into my thoughts with a question warmly spoken, "I believe the point of our journey is to help people *see Jesus*, isn't it?"

I smiled sheepishly, sure my face was red. "True, but you better pray for me, Silas. I don't know how much longer I can put up with traveling in circles." I tried to laugh but knew it sounded forced.

When we stopped for a rest, I noticed Silas take Paul aside. I couldn't catch everything that was said between them, but I did hear Silas say, "I don't know. I'm just warning you. He may turn out to be another John Mark."

Whoever John Mark was, it sounded as if Silas was afraid I would turn out just like him. While I didn't know what that meant, I could see the idea bothered Paul.

After a lunch of trout caught in the river and roasted over a quick fire, we continued northwest along the Phrygian Way. Sheep dotted the bare hills on both sides of our valley trail as we passed farms and small villages. The terrain became flatter and the hiking got easier. The presence of seagulls high above indicated water nearby. When we came to the outskirts of Troas, a city named by Alexander the Great, we made our last camp in Mysia. [28] As we laid out our bedrolls, Luke told us the Greek legend of the Trojan horse, the story of a battle in which the Greek army defeated the nearby city of Troy by sending them what looked like a present but what was in fact the source of their downfall.

Early the next day the golden sun peeked through the tree branches. In the distance a rooster crowed. Paul sat up on his blanket, greeted us with a big, bright smile, and joined our circle around the campfire. He looked more at ease than he had since early in our journey. "Last night, God gave me a vision," Paul said. "A man appeared before me and urged me to follow him into Macedonia."[29] He clapped his hands in enthusiasm, eyes sparkling. "I believe God used that vision to show us the way to go."[30]

Relieved, I grinned and joined the others in packing our limited gear. Within moments the team was headed down to the dock where we found a ship headed for Neapolis. Silas paid the skipper four shiny new drachma coins, and we boarded the vessel for the next leg of our journey—a journey that finally had a definite direction. As we left Troas and sailed toward the island of Samothrace,[31] I felt all my previous frustration fade away. My first time out on the water was more exciting than I had imagined.

Paul took me to the bow of the boat, and for a few minutes we simply stood shoulder to shoulder as I marveled over the dolphins and flying fish. Then Paul laid a hand on my arm and pointed out Mount Fengari straight ahead. I could hear the wind in the sail and the water beating against the hull. I could smell the algae and feel the saltwater breeze. Our vessel skimmed across the deep blue of the Aegean Sea with ease, and I smiled until my jaw hurt. Paul, it seemed, was finding as much joy in my reaction to the experience as I found in taking in the wonders around me.

Finally, deciding I should sit for a rest as I had no idea what might await me once we arrived, I moved to join the others. Paul had to steady me as I stumbled and struggled to find the rhythm of the bobbing decking below me.

We settled on a bench and Paul looked at me fondly. "Silas told me of your struggle with my earlier indecision," he began, "but I want you to know that I was never lost on our journey. I was merely waiting for the Lord to show me the way to go."

I wondered why he couldn't do that while resting in one place—preferably an exciting one—when he added, "I asked the Lord to direct us, and He did ... in His perfect timing."

I mumbled an apology for my complaints and what Paul had clearly seen as my gossiping about him. Then, when I was satisfied that my friend did not hold my poor choices against me, I asked him to tell me more about his Macedonian vision. His speculation that this was further confirmation that the Lord intended him to take the gospel to the Gentiles impressed me. How wonderful it must be to receive such communication straight from the Lord! I'd heard of God talking to Joseph, Samuel, and Daniel through dreams and visions, but I had always thought such revelations rare exceptions.

I decided to voice the question in my heart. "Do you think God might one day give me visions, Paul?"

"The Lord speaks primarily through His Word, Timothy. First look there for guidance. But know that He could certainly speak to you through a dream or vision or some other route should He choose to. God promised through Isaiah, 'Your ears shall hear a word behind you, saying, "This is the way, walk in it."'[32] That voice may come through different avenues, such as visions or circumstances, but it will always line up with God's Word revealed in Scripture.

"Take this call to go to the Macedonians, to focus my ministry on the Gentiles rather than the Jews. I know the Lord has been directing me this way for years, but at first I decided to weigh it against Scripture. And you know what I found?"

I shook my head no.

"I saw that while throughout history God has worked through His covenant people, the sons of Israel, He most certainly has a heart for Gentiles too. Just think of those He used! Rahab, an enemy prostitute, and Ruth, one of Israel's Moabite enemies descended from incest, were both woven into the lineage of David and thus of Christ! It's remarkable really."

I thought about what he shared. "Well, what if I don't know Scripture well enough to use it as the standard you're talking about? When I get an idea about something, how can I be sure I'm hearing God's voice and not my own thoughts ... or even the Devil's?"

"Timothy," Paul said with a grin, "how do you know *my* voice?"

"I guess I know the sound of your voice because I have spent time with you and have gotten to know you."

"You've answered your own question. Spend time with the Lord in prayer; study His Word, making it ever more familiar. You will learn to recognize His voice."[33]

"That seems to be a tall order."

"True," Paul nodded, "but we don't have to do it on our own."

"You mean I can count on you and the other believers to help me?"

He nodded, but then commented that there was more to the picture. "Timothy, when you became a Christian, you received the Holy Spirit. He, the Spirit of the Lord, abides within you—within all true believers, and He wants to lead you in the best paths. Jesus promised, 'The Helper, the Holy Spirit, whom the Father will send in My name, He will teach you all things.'[34] And so, the Holy Spirit directs us with intuition, illumination, knowledge, understanding, discernment, wisdom, a sensitive conscience, and even dreams and visions like last night's. It is also He who helps us recall God's Word."

I smiled. Perhaps my ability to so quickly memorize Scripture was a God-given gift. I wanted to know more. "What does it feel like to have the Spirit lead you?"

Paul smiled. "That is a deep question, Son. But in general I'd say that with the Spirit's direction comes a deep sensation of peace.[35] In fact, for the Christian, the presence of God's peace is an indication of the Spirit's leadership. And conversely, the lack of such peace is a sign of disobedience."[36]

That stung. I often felt conflicted inside, not at peace. I coughed to cover my discomfort, "So just follow your heart, huh?"

Paul's brow creased. "I wouldn't quite put it like that, because emotions can mislead. As Jeremiah says, 'The heart *is* deceitful above all *things*.'[37] The heart can play tricks on us. But if you are humble and submissive to the Lord, He will lead you. Christ's guidance is always available to those who ask for it."

Paul smiled, stood, and started toward the stern, undoubtedly planning to share the gospel with the sailors there. I stopped him just before he moved beyond me and asked, "Who's John Mark?"

Paul smiled knowingly. He realized I'd overheard his conversation with Silas, but he didn't seem to mind. "John Mark is a young man much like you. He went with us on our first missionary journey."

"And he decided to stay home for this one?"

Paul inhaled slowly, weighing his words. "I didn't ask him to come. Last time he left us and went home early."[38]

I looked down at the deck, hoping Paul couldn't tell that I'd contemplated doing that very thing. Thankfully, he strode away without further comment.

That day, as I stared across the water at the hazy horizon, I realized that while the path I'd chosen certainly had its highlights, long-term missionary service alone would not make me happy. In fact, at times it was anything but fun. Could it be that allowing the Holy Spirit to work in my heart would make me more at peace? More grateful for the high points in our journey and less irritable about the things I didn't particularly enjoy? Less likely to give in to anger?

I wasn't certain, but I realized enough about the Christian life that I knew the best way to find out was to step out in faith—in this case, to actively ask God to take control of my attitude by the power of His Holy Spirit, to lead me to peace. And then I'd listen. I'd listen to God's Word. I'd listen to Paul. And I'd take a good hard look at my heart. Perhaps I'd reach the point where I would know I was just where God wanted me to be.

Grow as a Disciple:

In this chapter, young Timothy sought to find his own way. Name the internal guide of every Christian._____

_____

In following God, what's more important: physical eyesight or faith? Why? _____

_____

Paul walked by faith. Describe a situation in which you acted out of faith. _____

_____

_____

If you have not already done so, please consider asking Jesus Christ to be Lord of your life. For more information, go to the appendix in the back of this book and read, "How to Know You Are a Christian."

Memory Verse:

Commit to memory either John 14:26 or Romans 8:6. Write it here for practice. _____

_____

_____

Prepare to Disciple Others:

Based on what you've read, how should you counsel a person who comes to you for basic life guidance? _____

_____

_____

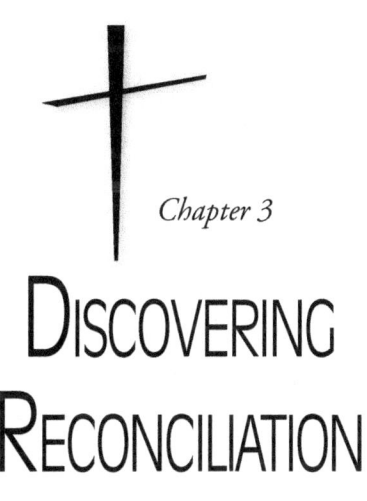

Chapter 3

DISCOVERING
RECONCILIATION

Our voyage across the Aegean Sea ended at the small, intercoastal village of Neapolis. After going ashore, we trekked ten miles further inland to the Roman colony of Philippi, slogging through the marshes as we went. The march through the swamp was slippery, and sightings of numerous water snakes kept me on edge. When we finally reached the solid ground of the city, I looked around in relief, hoping those people we encountered would not judge us too harshly for the filth that clung to our sandals and calves.

Built on the side of a hill under a massive rocky precipice, Philippi enjoyed abundant natural resources; the citizens had plenty of water, harvested timber, and even mined gold. The city was located in the northeast section of Macedonia and was named after Alexander the Great's father, Philip. According to Luke, the Romans once fought a civil war on the plains outside of town. After the battle, many army veterans retired in Philippi, giving the city an Italian flair.

On the evening of our first day in Philippi, I bathed in the river, bought some new clothes, and immediately felt better about myself. When I returned Silas's old garments, he noted that my muddy old sandals look tired and suggested I replace them while I could. So late the next morning, Luke and I separated from Paul and Silas so we could do a bit of shopping along the side streets of Philippi. Soon after Luke teamed up with us, I'd quickly realized the value of having four in our group: errands could be run without cutting into our time to evangelize. Further, working in pairs ensured none of us ever walked unfamiliar streets alone.

I stopped at the booth of a merchant who displayed on his rug a variety of sandals. I knelt and admired the leather craftsmanship, twisting and testing the quality. Just before I asked about the price of the footwear, I held up a sandal for Luke's inspection. He agreed it was fine. I stood up, mentally counting the coins in my pouch, when I saw a strange commotion happening further down the street near the agora.

As the assembled mob grew and people nearby scrambled away from potential danger, I decided the sandals would have to wait. I tossed them back to the rug, and Luke and I headed for the crowded central square. It quickly became apparent that the mob was gathered around two troublemakers, though I couldn't imagine what they could have done to cause such an uproar.

When we reached the outer edges of the crowd, I stood on my tiptoes, trying to get a glimpse of the faces of the men who had stirred up such chaos. I couldn't see, but Luke, who stood a bit taller, peered over the crowd and turned ashen. "God, help us," he pleaded. "They've got Paul and Silas!"

I gasped and watched Luke to see what he would do. When he hesitated to move into the fray, whether from his determination never to harm or from his advanced age, I bolted into the crowd and pushed my way into the mob, shoving my way through. Angry voices buzzed around me like droning bees around a busted hive, and I could barely hear Luke shouting my name. Sharp elbows gouged my side, and the shouts surrounding me were filled with hatred and venom. Some yelled, "They ought to leave us alone! We don't need their kind here!" Others demanded that the troublemakers undo whatever it was they'd done.[39] Clearly the gospel teaching Paul and Silas had intended to do in the city center had not gone over well.

Trying not to panic, I wormed my way closer to Paul and Silas. *Maybe I can defend them,* I thought wildly, *or help them escape.* But sheer terror stopped me in my tracks when I suddenly realized I could not breathe. I strained to get air into my lungs and began to panic as my brain registered that a long-fingered hand grasped the back of my neck and the collar of my tunic, pulling it taut against my throat. Like a charioteer yanking on his horse's reins, my captor jerked me backward, out of the crowd.

I soon discovered Luke was my attacker, though his eyes were filled not with anger toward me but with deep sorrow for our friends. "It is too risky," he said in a hushed tone, motioning that we must retreat to the safety of the home where we stayed.

For a moment, I felt a surge of rebellion and fierce rage. How could Luke just abandon our friends? I am certain my eyes blazed fire at him because the next thing I knew, gentle, white-haired Luke—the man who looked like a desert prophet of old—raised his walking stick as if to strike me. He still had me by the collar, and he said in his sternest voice, "We *cannot* help them, Timothy."

After a few more subdued protests, I finally abandoned my rescue heroics. Luke and I would listen and pray, and if Paul and Silas survived, we'd be ready to care for them.

Luke and I were at Lydia's house when we learned soldiers had eventually taken Paul and Silas to prison.[40] Lydia was the first person to trust Christ as Lord and Savior when we arrived in Philippi. Immediately after she and her family were baptized, she insisted our missionary team stay in her large home. We were happy to oblige her and thrilled to have a comfortable place to rest after so many weeks of travel.[41]

Lydia owned a lucrative textile business. She sold and traded fine purple linen, and she dressed in purple as well. Lydia always appeared refined and professional, wearing her graying hair up on her head with white pearls looped about in the shape of a tiara. Lydia was both a gracious lady and a splendid hostess, and she was wonderfully calming in the face of my panic. Still, even her best efforts at filling us with good food and soothing conversation failed to help me get to sleep that night.

"Timothy, you are pacing back and forth like a leopard in a cage," Luke complained. "Please, lie down!"

I'd been on and off my sleeping pallet for hours, desperately wishing there were something I could do for Paul and Silas. "We've just got to get them out of jail, Luke!" I insisted in a loud whisper. In spite of my pacing and worry, there was no need to wake the household.

"We'll deal with it tomorrow, in the daylight," Luke soothed. "In the meantime, pray."

I lay down, but couldn't sleep. I tossed and turned, sending up prayers and worrying at the same time. Finally, sleep claimed me.

I had just begun to dream when a terrible grinding, rumbling sound woke me. I sat up, startled, as the house began to shake violently. Luke told me to cover my head as cracks began to snake up the walls, earthen pots toppling from their shelves throughout the house and shattering as they hit the floor. The ground beneath our pallets moved up and down, like the deck of a storm-tossed ship. The earthquake rattled everything in Lydia's house.[42]

As soon as I could, I scrambled to my feet and helped Luke rise.

Moments later, from another room, Lydia's voice rang out through the night. "We are safe and unharmed. Are you gentlemen alright?"

I answered her. "Yes, we are fine, thank you … just a little shaken." I lit a lamp that had escaped damage. It appeared to be the only thing in the room that had survived unscathed. The mess would need to be addressed in the light of day.

A sudden realization gripped me. "Paul and Silas are still in the jailhouse," I shouted. "They may be hurt!"

Though we had no idea whether we could reach our friends and plenty of reason to believe they may have been killed during the earthquake, the two of us hastily dressed, called out thanks to Lydia's family, and rushed into the night. I led the way, having carefully questioned one of Lydia's sons for directions to the jail earlier in the day. Luke followed.

My heart pounded as we walked quickly through the dark streets.

Rivers of adrenaline raced through my veins, my tension rising when I realized distant screams and wails were beginning to fill the night. How many were injured in the earthquake? Killed?

When we finally arrived at our destination, I noticed right away that the prison building was falling to ruins. The main door was wide open, so we entered without asking permission. Inside I could see, by light of a lone torch hanging perilously from its place on the wall, that the whole structure was filled with gaping holes and cracks. Unless the men held inside had been killed, I suspected, many of the prisoners easily could emerge to freedom. Likely several had already escaped into the night.

Luke, still trying to catch his breath after our journey, stated the obvious. "Th-they may have been cr-crushed to death. All the w-walls and pillars are stone. The prisoners are held below this level."

I frowned. "Let's go," I said. We stepped over piles of rock and rubble as we descended deep into the black heart of the dungeon, using a central stone staircase that was lit by torches and appeared fairly stable in spite of the general destruction on the main floor. The lower we went, the stronger the foul odor hanging in the air grew: the place reeked of decay and disease. Finally, from out of the darkness, we heard the faint sound of voices coming from just ahead of us. "There are still men here!" Luke said with a rush of relief. "Paul and Silas may be alive yet!"

I pressed forward, thankful to see torchlight flickering far up ahead at the end of what looked like a long, wide corridor. Within moments Luke and I had drawn closer to the distant flame. Luke stumbled into me when I nearly tripped over something large on the floor. It had been disguised by the deep shadows. For a moment I feared I'd run into a dead body, but then I heard a moan. It came from a man in noisy Roman armor, judging by the sound made when he moved.

"It's the jailer," Luke said, bending to check him for signs of injury as I hoped the man's sword wasn't nearby. Who knew what he might do to us? "Help is here, friend. Tell me, what can I do for you?"

To my surprise, the man let out a sob and began spilling his story, apparently unconcerned why two strangers had wandered into his jail in the middle of the night. He'd been guarding the prisoners, listening to the two newest arrivals talk of salvation through Jesus and singing joyfully in their cell, when the earth began to rumble and total chaos ensued. "I guess I'd drifted to sleep to the sound of their singing," he said. "And just as I came to, all the prison doors flew open and everyone's chains fell off!"

I listened intently, noticing for the first time that the jail was still full. I could hear the murmurs of many voices surrounding me, perhaps commenting on the story they could surely hear the jailer relate. Eerily, not one called out or approached us, though I had no doubt the rumbling had indeed opened or broken the doors to their cells.

"I drew my sword," he reported, "and I was just about to kill myself over this disaster—knowing my superiors would demand my life in place of the escapees—when one of those newest inmates shouted at me: 'Do yourself no harm, for we are all here.'"[43] The jailer began to cry. "How," he asked Luke, "did he know what I planned? Surely he could not see what I was doing over here in the darkness."

I could hear the smile in Luke's voice. "You are unharmed, friend. Please, bring us more light, and we will see this prisoner you speak of. He is our brother, and none of us will hurt you. If you'll let us, we will help you."

The jailer scrambled up off the floor while we continued forward. There, in a cell complete with stocks and chains, we found Paul and Silas. They were alive, but it didn't take Luke long to discover their backs were raw. Silas, clearly in pain, admitted they had been beaten mercilessly with bamboo canes. Their tunics were ripped beyond repair, and their backs were crisscrossed with deep red lines. After careful examination, Luke winced and shook his head. They needed medical attention.

The jailer, bearing a torch, secured the prison's cell doors as he returned. Remarkably, not one prisoner challenged him, though it seemed all had survived uninjured.

"Do you have any medical supplies here?" Luke asked as the jailer drew near.

"No," he replied, "but my home is next door. Come, we will go there. I have oil, wine, and bandages."

Luke moved to follow him, but the jailer did something strange. He went to Paul, leaned down to him, and helped him stand. When it was clear he meant to assist us in taking Paul and Silas out of the jail, I felt my shoulders sag with relief. When I heard him ask Paul and Silas, "Sirs, what must I do to be saved?"[44] I nearly wept with joy.

We followed the jailer back down the corridor, up the stairs, and through the darkness, listening for the jangling sound of the keys on his belt. Outside the fresh night air felt cool, and I was relieved when he allowed us to sit on benches in his small courtyard rather than asking us to enter his home. No doubt that structure too was compromised. Within moments of our arrival, both his wife and children—ranging in age from six to sixteen—had joined us, medical supplies in hand.

Luke approached Paul as soon as he had the oil and bandages, ready to work on his wounds, but Paul motioned him to wait. Then, with his back still bleeding and the stink of prison on him, Paul spoke. "Listen to me," he said to the jailer, having found renewed strength in the fresh air, "and I will teach you—and your family—how to be saved."

"Saved from what, sir?" the jailer's wife asked timidly. I could not imagine how tense she must be over the night's events.

"From the stain of sin or wrongdoing," Paul clarified. "When you trust Christ as your Savior, He forgives your sin[45] and gives you eternal life."[46]

The jailer and his family were wide-eyed for the next several minutes as Paul began sharing his testimony. "I am a new creation today; you have nothing to fear from me. But I behaved like a wretch before I met the Lord," he admitted. "I persecuted the followers of Jesus and tried to destroy their gatherings.[47] But one day while I was traveling on the road to Damascus, the risen Jesus appeared to me in a brilliant light and asked, 'Why are you persecuting Me?'[48] Up to that point, I considered Jesus a deluded rabbi who was nothing more than a rabble-rouser. But then I saw Him: The Christ who was supposed to be dead was alive and talking to me directly from heaven! I was blinded temporarily by the experience, but spiritually speaking I was beginning to see more clearly than ever." He smiled, hardly letting on that he was in pain. Only his slouch and the strain around his eyes gave him away.

"They led me by the hand into Damascus," he continued. "Three days later a man named Ananias came to me there and encouraged me to pray. That very day I turned away from my sin, trusted Christ as my Savior, and was baptized. Ever since then I am a new man—free, even when in chains."

Paul closed his eyes, face upturned toward heaven and exclaimed, "Hallelujah! Though I have been the chief of sinners, because of Christ's crucifixion, I can enjoy reconciliation with my Lord!"[49]

The jailer looked puzzled. "Reconciliation? Please, sir. What does it mean?"

Paul's face brightened in the moonlight. "Reconciliation happens when two estranged parties come together in peace. This is why innocent Jesus died on a cross, so we who were guilty could be reconciled to God.[50] We were far away from God and separated from Him because of our sins, but Jesus brought us together in peace.[51] Christ reconciled us to God,[52] restoring us to right relationship with Him."

Luke once again moved behind Paul, oil and bandages tucked under his arm, but Paul waved him away. He was not finished with his teaching. "When you trust in the substitutionary work of Christ," he said to the jailer, "you change from God's enemy to God's friend."

The jailer frowned, looked down, and then finally sat up straight and crossed his arms over his chest. "I don't know about that," he said. "I'm not so certain Creator God would ever forgive a man like me."

Paul's voice gentled, "But that is just what He wants to do for you! Jesus went to the cross so you would not have to experience God's judgment. Jesus took your punishment upon Himself and died in your place.[53] Forgiveness and reconciliation are yours for the taking."

"But I have done *horrible* things," the jailer cried, quickly confessing a list of crimes including murder, forced-starvation, torture, and other unspeakable atrocities.

As I listened to the man's candid confession, I was sickened. But as

I noticed the jailer's wife and children listening, their eyes bulging and their lips separating in disbelief and horror, I realized how important it was that my face show no judgment for the jailer but only love. In truth, his sins were no more offensive to the Lord than my own. I was a scrappy brawler when I met Christ, and I still struggled with old habits—even though I knew I was forgiven.

The jailer wrung his hands and looked up at Paul, "Sir, again I ask, what must I do to be saved?"[54]

Paul answered. "The gospel of Christ brings salvation to everyone who believes.[55] But first, you have to understand that no one is righteous, not one.[56] No one is perfect: not me, Silas, Luke, not even handsome young Timothy over there." Paul threw me a glance. Then he turned to appeal to the jailer and his family, his voice warm and kind. "All have sinned and come short of the glory of God.[57] But though the wages of our sins is death, the gift of God is eternal life through Jesus Christ our Lord.[58] God, you see, demonstrated His love toward you in that while you were still a sinner, Christ died for you.[59] Not because of anything good in you, but because of His love for you.

"God's kindness," he finished as they listened intently, "is meant to lead you to repentance.[60] The Lord wants you to change your mind and change your direction. Turn away from your sin, and turn to Christ." Then in a softer tone Paul pleaded, "If you confess with your mouth Jesus as Lord and believe in your heart God raised Him from the dead, you will be saved.[61] For everyone who calls on the name of the Lord will be saved."[62] He paused and then asked the jailer, "Are you ready to receive God's free gift of eternal life?"

"Yes sir, I want to go to heaven," the man replied. "From now on I will be a better person. I promise! I will be nicer to the prisoners. And I will …"

Wrong answer, I thought to myself.

Paul interrupted him, explaining again that forgiveness is a *gift* from God—received by faith, never to be earned by good works.[63] But the poor jailer was confused. My heart beat faster, and I wanted to testify, to help him understand.

"Excuse me, Paul," I broke in. "May I share a few Scriptures with our friends?"

With Paul's nod of approval I began, "Many years ago, my grandmother taught me these Scriptures[64] that may help explain. Listen to what the Prophets say—and notice that salvation is never tied to good works." Then I rapidly rattled off verses, careful to use inflection and pauses as I had so often heard Paul do. "The Hebrew prophet Isaiah said, 'Though your sins are like scarlet, they shall be as white as snow; though they are red like crimson, they shall be as wool.'[65] The prophet Micah said God will 'cast all our sins into the depths of the sea.'[66] God said through Jeremiah, 'I will forgive their iniquity, and their sin I will remember no more.'[67] And King David of old said, 'As far as the east is from the west, so far has He removed our transgressions from us.'"[68]

Silas broke in, summing up our explanation in his typically brief way. "To accept God's free gift of salvation, all you have to do is trust in what Christ has done for you on the cross."[69]

Paul affirmed, "Christ will take your sin and give you His righteousness.[70] Forgiveness is only a prayer away."

Explaining that he finally understood, the jailer started to weep and reached for his wife's hand. She leaned into him, and Luke and I rose and stepped into the shadows to give them more privacy. As I heard the soldier and his family accept Christ as Lord, I rejoiced. But I also was saddened by what I'd heard the man confess. No wonder the poor fellow struggled with the idea of undeserved forgiveness.

I wandered to the farthest reaches of the courtyard, realizing I too struggled with the concept of forgiveness but in a different way. I struggled to forgive my father. His selfishness had devastated my mother and made Hitty bitter. It had imprisoned me in anger, and I wanted out. Yet no matter how often I told myself I forgave Achilles son of Odysseus, old memories haunted me. Father had made horrible mistakes with our family. How could God expect me to forgive him?

I ran both hands through my hair, looked up at the stars, and muttered, "Oh, God. Help."

Luke, standing across the wide courtyard, approached at the sound of my voice as the others prayed far behind us. "What is it, Timothy?" he asked kindly.

"My father's sins against my family," I whispered.

"And have you forgiven him as the Lord forgave you?"[71]

"I've tried," I huffed.

"Jesus taught we must forgive others seven times seventy times—meaning as often as necessary.[72] He knows that for humans, extending forgiveness is not always a onetime event but must be reinforced through determination to release hurt." He sighed and slipped an arm around my shoulders; he'd heard my life story. "You must forgive your father. Release him from the debt of wrong he committed against you. Not because he deserves it, but because it reflects what the Lord has done for us—what He would like to do for your father."

Luke prayed for me, then quietly walked away, leaving me to have a long talk with God as the jailer—remarkably—rose from his confession of faith and personally washed and bandaged the wounds my friends had sustained.

Just as the sun began to rise, I heard a bird let out its first cheerful greeting of the morning from the nearby bushes. I looked up from the wooden bench where I knelt and saw the morning star in the eastern sky. In my heart, I sensed a spiritual breakthrough. There in the jailer's courtyard, my heart was reconciled with my father, possibly for the first time.

As the city began to wake, we all walked down to the river for an unforgettable sunrise baptism as the jailer and his entire household publicly acknowledged Jesus as their Lord and Savior. Then the family treated us to a hearty breakfast back at their house.[73]

While we ate, I sat and reflected on the events of the past twenty-four hours. The weeks of wilderness wanderings seemed a small price to pay when compared to the excitement, adventure, and joy I'd experienced during our tumultuous visit to Philippi. I wondered how I would ever return to farming.

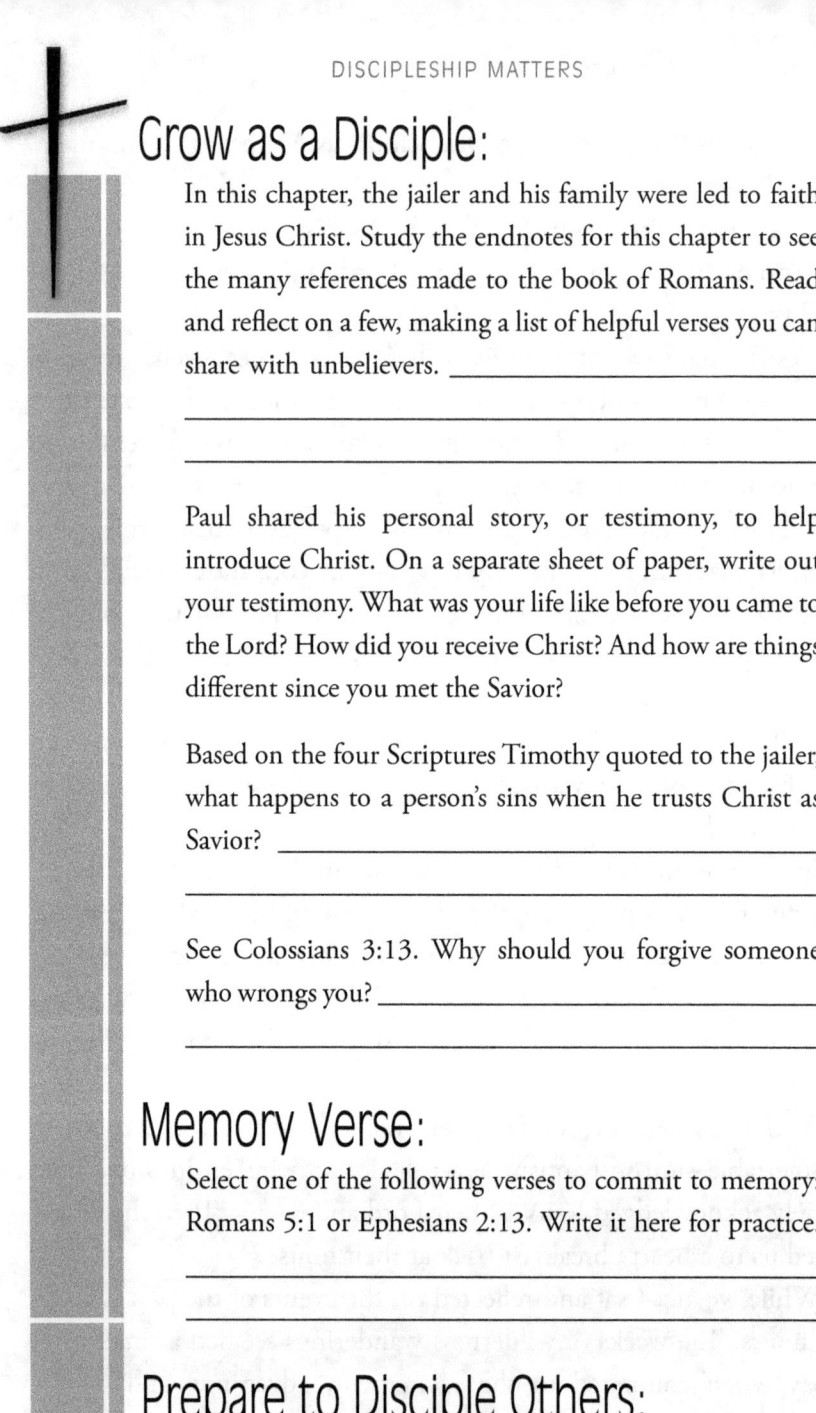

Grow as a Disciple:

In this chapter, the jailer and his family were led to faith in Jesus Christ. Study the endnotes for this chapter to see the many references made to the book of Romans. Read and reflect on a few, making a list of helpful verses you can share with unbelievers. _____

_____

_____

Paul shared his personal story, or testimony, to help introduce Christ. On a separate sheet of paper, write out your testimony. What was your life like before you came to the Lord? How did you receive Christ? And how are things different since you met the Savior?

Based on the four Scriptures Timothy quoted to the jailer, what happens to a person's sins when he trusts Christ as Savior? _____

_____

See Colossians 3:13. Why should you forgive someone who wrongs you? _____

_____

Memory Verse:

Select one of the following verses to commit to memory: Romans 5:1 or Ephesians 2:13. Write it here for practice.

_____

_____

Prepare to Disciple Others:

What would you say if someone asked you, "How can I have peace with God?" _____

_____

Chapter 4

DISCOVERING
CHRIST'S ATTITUDE

The following day the Philippian officials came to the prison where Paul and Silas had returned after the jailer's baptism, and they apologized.[74] They claimed they did not know Paul and Silas were Roman citizens when they beat and imprisoned them—as if that excused the mistreatment.[75] After the missionaries were released, we all went and said good-bye to the jailer and his family, to Lydia, and to the other new Christians. With words of encouragement, we committed them all to the care of the Lord[76] and warned them about Nicolas DoM and others like him.

We left Philippi, walking southwest along the *Via Egnatia*, an ancient Roman highway. The road contained many smooth stones placed into the earth, grass growing up among them. This major east-west route was twenty feet wide and stretched over a thousand miles in length. It connected the western and eastern parts of the Roman Empire, and we made good use of it.

The Romans are superb road builders, placing the pathways so that they are highest in the middle and water can roll off their gentle slopes and into the drainage ditches running alongside them. Normally, the Roman roads are straight in order to keep the distance between two points as short as possible and to give bandits fewer curves to hide behind. But the road out of Philippi is not normal. It curves out of the steep valley and winds through a forest of cyprus trees.

We were tired that morning. Paul and Silas were still weak from their beating as we hiked up a steep grade. Our steps were short and heavy, and our breathing was labored and difficult by the time we made it to the highest point along the road. Still, Paul urged us onward. If he was in pain, he didn't admit it.

Around noon I fell into step beside Paul and asked him about the jailer's report that he and Silas had been singing in their prison stocks.

"The joy of the Lord is our strength,"[77] Paul commented. "Singing helps me remember that when times look bleak."

Could I sing with joy in similar circumstances? I wondered. Not likely. "Well, I admire you for doing that. I'm not sure how you and Silas were able to maintain joy during all you went through, singing or not."

Paul stopped, motioning to the others that he wanted to take a quick break. Everyone stepped off the trail eagerly, and Paul led me over to a patch of dried grass. He knelt gingerly, asking me to do the same. Then he asked me to clear the grass so we could use the bare earth as a writing surface. Intrigued, I obeyed.

Paul grabbed a stubby stick and began to draw in the dust. As he'd done the night we were robbed, he drew first one circle, then another below it. Again he drew a line to connect the two.

"Tell me what this represents," Paul said.

"This top circle represents Christ, and this lower circle represents me."

He nodded, retracing the line between the circles. "When the Lord arose from the dead and ascended back into heaven, He then sent His Spirit to come down to His followers. That Spirit is our strength for life. He is the source of my joy and my stability in a weary world. We can have the mind of Christ, Son. Because Christ reigns in us, we can share His attitude—even when we suffer." He squeezed his problem eye closed in a wink and smiled at me. "When Jesus expresses His nature through a man, his attitude improves."

Before I had the chance to ask further questions, our attention was drawn to the sound of Roman soldiers approaching. The nails in the bottom of their special sandals, known as *caligae*, clicked against the road's surface, a fearsome noise. We moved further back from the road and found a comfortable place to sit under the shade of a willow tree as the long line of what looked like giant red ants marched right past us. This was just the kind of sight I'd so longed to see, though I hoped they'd leave us alone.

First in line came the standard bearers. They held high their colors and ensign. One even held a silver eagle on a pole. Another standard bearer wore a lion head over his helmet. Next came the Roman foot soldiers, wearing red tunics that stopped just above their knees. The armor across their chests and shoulders flashed in the sunlight, and large leather belts hugged their waists. From one side of their belts hung daggers and from the other side hung long swords. In their left hands, each soldier held an oblong shield, and in his right hand, he carried his spear. Red capes were draped over their shoulders, looking a little worse for wear. I noticed they also wore *greaves* to protect their shins and helmets designed to protect their heads, necks, and faces. The individual soldiers, I realized, were a curious mixture of young and old. Some had leathery faces; others were as smooth-cheeked as my sister. I didn't know where they were going or what they were doing, but I knew I'd never forget that parade of warriors.

When the legion passed, we dusted ourselves off and got back on the road again. "Tell me more about this attitude of Christ, please," I said to Paul. "Exactly what attitudes are of Him?"

"Christ's Spirit at work in us generates love, joy, peace, patience, kindness, goodness, faithfulness, gentleness, and self-control,"[78] Paul said without preamble. Then he looked at me, his expression thoughtful. "But if you find those things missing in your life at times, remember the Lord's words: 'If anyone thirsts, let him come to Me and drink.'"[79]

I raised a questioning eyebrow.

"In other words," he clarified, "don't be complacent or self-reliant.

Tell the Lord you are thirsty for Him, His presence, His Spirit. Seek His help."

I hung my head, aware of how many times I failed to go to God with my bad attitude, instead allowing it to leak out over others. "I do seek His help, Paul," I insisted. "But sometimes I feel so ashamed of my failures when I think of God's command in Leviticus. 'Be holy; for I am holy,'"[80] I sighed heavily. "I know my sins are unholy.[81] I wonder if I can ever be the man Christ wants me to be."

Paul ignored my defeatist attitude. "Holiness is never optional because sin always upsets God.[82] If a Christian transgresses, he must agree with God about his sin and request His forgiveness[83] as David did when he prayed, 'Wash me thoroughly from my iniquity, and cleanse me from my sin.'"[84]

"I do those things," I said, trying not to sound defensive.

"Good," he affirmed. "But a Christian who wants to walk in the fullness of the Spirit must continually yield to the Lord.[85] Everyday he must say no to self, and say yes to God."

Our conversation paused briefly as the darkening western horizon drew our attention. Big clouds swirled in the heavens, a few birds flying high and silent overhead. A flash of lightning streaked across the sky as the atmospheric pressure changed. And then, almost immediately, the air grew still, heavy.

"Should we seek shelter?" Luke, a few paces behind us, asked.

Paul said it was early yet and continued on, oblivious when the rain began to fall on our heads in fat drops. "As Christians," he said to me, "You have two forces within you—an old nature and a new nature.[86] The old nature, inherited from the first man Adam, is the selfish and sinful part of you. But you also have a new nature. The Spirit within you, a blessing inherited from Jesus, is gracious and wonderful. You must decide daily which nature you want to follow, your old nature or the new nature. The old nature always wants to reassert itself." [87]

"But how do I suppress the old flesh nature?" I stared down at my feet. "Paul, I feel as if I even sin in my sleep some days."

I thought I heard Silas snicker behind me. He'd told me I once punched the air in my sleep, but I'd thought he was joking. Perhaps he hadn't made up the story; that was unlike him.

"You must exercise your will," Paul insisted. "You must tell God your sincere desire to be controlled by His Spirit. Jesus promised the Heavenly Father wants to give the Holy Spirit to those who ask Him.[88] So just ask and trust that He hears you."

The rain began to fall harder, so we didn't notice the approach of another small band of Roman soldiers until the eight-man *contubernium* overtook us. These fellows seemed to have just returned from battle— or perhaps from harassing some poor souls. Their faces were dirty, their eyes were heavy, and they looked mean.

I tried not to show any reaction when the last man in the group pointed at me and demanded that I carry his *sarcina*, a pack filled with food and camp supplies that weighed at least fifty pounds. "Boy," he said as if I were eight and not eighteen, "that sack is your responsibility for the next mile. Drop it, and I'll drop you flat." But when one of the soldiers with him turned and assessed me as well, his lip curling in disgust over something about me that he found lacking, I had to pray hard that the Lord would let His Spirit shine through me. Without His help, I surely would've caused a scene before I agreed to carry the heavy pack. And that, I knew from stories, could prove deadly.

The rain started to fall in sheets. A gust of wind came up suddenly, and a loud crack of thunder rang out overhead. "We will wait for you at the next junction," Silas said to me, signaling with a jerk of his head that I should follow the soldiers quickly.

I obeyed as the downpour pelted me, thoroughly soaking my clothing. I knew the hike ahead would be long with the Roman company being cranky and the extra weight straining my back muscles. Still, I leaned heavily on Paul's earlier teaching that the ability to rejoice requires the proper choice. *I will accept this challenge with the right spirit,* I told myself as the wind pushed us forward. The driving force against my back almost seemed an affirmation that I would indeed allow the Holy Spirit to propel me.

"I'll carry the bag for two miles, sir,"[89] I called up to the soldier who'd thrown his burden to me.

In the rain, the soldier turned, and while he did not smile, I thought I saw surprise and a hint of relief in his expression. No telling how far the men had traveled or what they had endured.

I wiped the rain from my face with the back of my arm and offered a silent prayer: *God, I don't want to be a complainer, so I must have Your help. I surrender myself to You, Lord, and ask You to fill me with Your precious Holy Spirit. Please give me Your joy, peace, and patience. Let Your nature shine through me.*

As I labored down the road under the weight of the pack, I picked up my feet so as not to slip on the wet smooth stones. Remarkably, I found fresh courage and joy in spite of the circumstances. After about a half mile, I even managed to hum a tune of praise.

By the time we'd reached the first mile marker, the soldier whose pack I carried had slowed his pace to walk alongside me, perhaps curious about my joyful tune in such a miserable circumstance. "I am Fortunatus," he offered, and though he did not thank me when I kept walking rather than dropping his pack at the point required, he did start up a conversation.

I learned where he'd been and where they were headed. He told me about his family, of the wife who lay at home sick. And I told him of Jesus, the healer, the Messiah who loved him and who cared about his wife, his troubles, and his future.

Though the other soldiers occasionally looked back at us as if I were mad, Fortunatus listened intently. When we reached mile marker two, the rain passed and the sun came out, and I kept walking.

"I need to know this Jesus," my new friend finally said.

And by the time we parted ways, Fortunatus had become my brother in the Lord.

Grow as a Disciple:

Paul explained to Timothy that through living life in the Spirit, we can maintain an outlook that reflects Christ's character. Do you think being filled with the Spirit means getting more of Him or allowing Him to have more of you? Explain._____

_____

_____

Is there ever a time when you don't need to be led by the Spirit? Why or why not? _____

_____

What does a person have to do to be filled with the Spirit? _____

_____

How do you know when Jesus is expressing His character through you? _____

_____

Memory Verse:

Select either Galatians 5:22-23 or Ephesians 5:18 to commit memory. Write it here for practice. _____

_____

_____

Prepare to Disciple Others:

How might you encourage a Christian frustrated by circumstances? What would you encourage her to pray? Explain your reasoning. _____

_____

_____

Chapter 5

DISCOVERING CHRIST'S POWER

For a hundred miles after Fortunatus and I parted ways, the other missionaries and I continued west along the *Via Egnatia.* We finally stopped in Thessalonica. Named after the stepsister of Alexander the Great, Thessalonica was the capital of the Roman province of Macedonia, the heart of the area to which Paul was called in his vision. The city would become a strategic location from which to spread the gospel, for it was located on the all-important east-to-west highway and enjoyed access to a busy harbor on the Aegean Sea.

Our ministry in Thessalonica began at the local synagogue, where Paul read from the Scriptures to contend with the Jews that Jesus was in fact their long-awaited Messiah.[90] Early into the meeting, our hearts felt light because the message was received by many. But not all efforts proved so fruitful. When a sensitive issue arose within the local body of believers, some of our evangelistic energies were redirected to church business.

The early church as a whole was largely known for its generosity: believers shared meals, opened their homes, and gave to those in need. But a few unethical people in Thessalonica began to take advantage of this quality in the church family. Some believers began to rely so heavily on handouts that they stopped working altogether! So to discourage slothfulness, Paul instituted the "no work, no eat rule."[91] And even though the church should have supported us in our Christian ministry, providing for us as Lydia had, Paul thought it best for our group of four to set an example in the matter of work ethic.

He returned to his tent-making trade, and Luke set up a medical practice. Burly Silas found work as a timber cutter—a job I found ironic given that his name meant "of the forest." I soon found a job with a smith. My responsibility was smelting the iron ore.

The job was hot and taxing. Each day I shoveled the coal, worked the bellows, and kept the bloomery hot. Then I forged welded ingots into billets. The heat, sweat, and rising blisters on my skin left me exhausted at the end of every day, but earning money and learning a new craft kept me motivated. When I had the time to stand back and observe the busyness around me, I marveled as I watched the artisans strike the anvil with loud and mighty blows, creating beautiful and useful metal objects. It amazed me that the Lord had placed metal ores in the heart of the earth, providing resources that could be harvested and repurposed in so many important ways.

For three weeks the others and I worked night and day to support ourselves.[92] Because we were so busy, there was little discretionary time to go and talk to people about Jesus. Instead, we learned to see each day as an opportunity to talk about the gospel as we went about our assigned tasks. Paul shared Christ while making tents. Luke shared Christ while practicing medicine. Silas shared Christ with the other workmen in the forest. And I shared Christ in the forge, quickly finding that our brief lunch breaks provided plenty of chances to share truth. All the long hours in Thessalonica were well worth it as we saw a few Jews; many Gentiles; and even some wealthy, prominent ladies profess faith in Christ.[93] In spite of our time and energy limitations, the Lord used our witness to such an extent that even those who did not patronize our businesses heard the good news through those with whom we shared.

Sadly, some unbelieving Jews became jealous of the success the message of Christ found among the people. They hired a group of thugs to incite a citywide riot.[94] They claimed we were turning the world upside down, but we knew we were turning it right side up, spreading the good news of God's kingdom as the Lord had charged us.

Not long after the ruckus broke out, the local believers insisted we leave town. "But stay off the highway," they warned. "Those who war against you will be watching the road."

Luke and I began our escape late that afternoon, darting like shadows through the narrow and dark streets. As we hurried along, we kept our faces down. Then, once out of town, we eased our efforts to be secretive and followed the trail toward the swamp. Our instructions were to go west and wait at the first bridge.

Later, under the cover of blackest night, Paul and Silas joined us.[95] An unlikely guide, a skinny fair-haired boy named Moshe, who allegedly knew the area better than anyone, came with them to lead us through the swamp. He and his dog took us down to the water's edge. The brush there was thick, and the air was hot and humid. Mosquitos buzzed by the millions. I hoped Moshe did not plan to make us wade through the mess that lay ahead.

The dog bumped up against my leg and I startled. "We could go through here," Moshe said to Paul. "It's not very deep. But we can walk around it too. Lots of snakes out there."

Luke wasted no time giving his opinion. "Let's walk around."

Several times that night we stopped while Moshe called his dog, who seemed to think our journey a grand adventure. We'd wait for him, getting swarmed by insects, until out of nowhere the enthusiastic hound would reappear and we would continue our trek. When we finally reached the other side of the swamp and headed toward the mountain town of Berea, I was covered in itchy bites and thrilled to see a town again. My companions never complained, but I figured they were as exhausted by the journey as I was.

The Bereans, we found, welcomed us and the gospel with open arms and hearts.[96] In their city, the ministry flourished until some hate-filled men back in Thessalonica got word of our whereabouts. Unbelievably, they traveled the fifty miles to Berea just to cause more trouble.[97] Through falsehoods, innuendo, and raw emotion, the same group of dissenters worked the crowds to convince them we were troublemakers. When the situation became untenable, the brothers insisted Paul—always targeted as our leader—sail for Athens.[98]

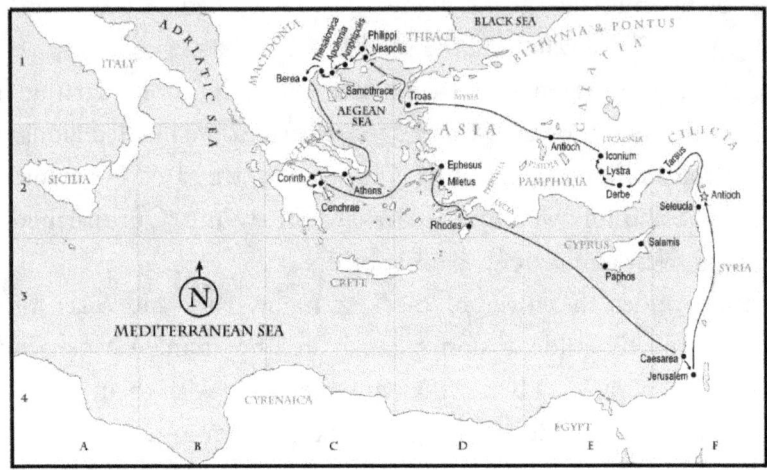

Paul, with Luke, agreed to move on, leaving me and Silas to continue the work in Berea under a lower profile. "We will soon rendezvous in Athens," Paul assured me just before they left. "In the meantime, I want you to watch how Silas serves. Soon *you* may be in a leadership role. The time may come when we must each travel separately."

I thought about his words long after our friends were gone, proudly telling myself Paul would not put such expectations on me were he not sure I could handle them. How much I'd grown since our departure from Lystra so many months ago! My head swelled a bit at the thought.

Silas and I laid low for a couple of days before we began quietly stabilizing the young ministry in Berea, discipling the existing Christ followers rather than focusing the bulk of our energy on evangelism. (Ideally, the Bereans would soon begin to evangelize their own people.) Teaching the Bereans more about Jesus and building their faith turned out to be a joy. They tended to be fair-minded people. All we had to do was point them to the Scriptures, and they would carefully examine the Law and Prophets to see for themselves that Jesus was the promised Messiah.

Later, as planned, Silas and I left the city to travel to Athens. Once we rejoined Paul, Silas gave him a complete report on the status of the church in Berea. Paul praised their noble character, impressed that the Berean believers had welcomed our teaching by daily weighing it against God's Word. [99]

I expected Paul to tell us how we could best serve with him and Luke in Athens, so I was surprised when he announced his plan to continue on to the great city of Corinth. More shocking was his announcement that Silas, alone, was to go back and make inroads into Amphipolis and Apollonia because Paul regretted that we did not stop in those places when we passed by them. [100] But I felt my heart swell with excitement over the next thing he said. "Timothy, I want you to go back to Macedonia. Silas will drop you off in Thessalonica en route to his own assignment. I'm concerned about the believers there. We left so quickly."

I wanted to shout for joy, but before I could respond, Silas—usually quiet—blurted, "You can't send Timothy there by himself!" [101]

Paul frowned, but then his eyes twinkled and his lips twitched under his mustache. I would later realize that he knew Silas's outburst signaled his growing affection for me: we'd become close friends. "Timothy will be fine," Paul said. "He will be less conspicuous there than you or me."

"But Thessalonica is dangerous," Silas blustered, looking more upset than I'd ever seen him. "We were fortunate to get out of there alive!"

I listened to Silas's objection, but ended up letting my pride and that old problem of anger get the best of me. "I can speak for myself, Silas," I retorted.

Luke joined in, looking first at me and then at Paul in concern. "Silas is right. That place is too perilous for one person—especially one as young as our friend Timothy."

Like a referee at a boxing match, Paul stepped forward until he was directly in the middle of our circle. He turned to look me full in the face. "Timothy, how do *you* feel about going to Thessalonica?"

"I'm not afraid," I said.

Paul smiled, asked the others to excuse us, and motioned for me to follow him up the Acropolis, the highest point of the city situated just above the tree line. On top of the hill stood the Parthenon, its white columns reaching up into the cobalt sky. The temple to the goddess Athena would have been beautiful, were it not a monument to idolatry.

When we stopped to catch our breath, Paul said, "Silas and Luke are right to be concerned for you. If you accept this assignment, you must take care. It could place you in grave danger."

I knew he referred to troublemakers like those based in Thessalonica and Nicolas DoM, whom we hadn't seen since the day Paul dealt with him along the trail. "Like I said," I insisted, "I'm not afraid. I'm ready to go. I can do anything you ask of me."

Hundreds of years earlier, the Athenian philosophers Plato, Socrates, and Aristotle taught from the hilltop where we stood. Their wisdom came from man's ideas below. But in the next moments, Paul began to share with me timely wisdom from above.[102] Unfortunately, I didn't much care for it.

"In truth," my mentor said, "you are not fully prepared for this experience."

I felt myself stiffen.

"But I've decided it would be good for you anyway."

"Wh-why send me if you think I can't handle it?" I stammered, feeling the rise of defensive anger. "Maybe I should just go home."

Paul smiled, and I tried not to notice the weary new lines around his eyes. "Nobody said anything about anyone going home," he soothed. "I just want you to realize what I'm really asking of you."

I tried to relax, breathing deeply and trying to pray for the Holy Spirit's help as I'd been taught.

"You see," he said, "the way we grow as Christians is by trying new things—finding new ways to step out in obedience. And as we do, we discover how inadequate we are, and that humbling experience pushes us into the arms of Jesus."

I nodded. I'd heard variations of this before during our travels.

"You never really experience the power of God until you come to the end of yourself," he continued. "When you realize you are insufficient and repent of the sin of self-sufficiency, you will then turn to God who is all-sufficient. And when you do, you'll find it is He who makes you sufficient."

My eyes narrowed. "So you *are* saying I'm inadequate?"

Paul sighed. "I am saying, 'Cursed is the man who trusts in man and makes flesh his strength.'[103] The fact is, Timothy, you don't have what it takes to be a missionary."

My face fell, sure that Paul was calling me a failure and deeply saddened because I knew I'd been giving my best and then some in the last weeks. Was I not enough?

Paul came closer and wrapped an arm around my sagging shoulders. "Don't grow so discouraged, Son. I don't have what it takes to be a missionary either. It's only God living in us that makes us adequate. Remember, He instructed His disciples not to leave Jerusalem until the Holy Spirit arrived to serve as their Helper."[104]

"So I've failed?" I managed to ask. "I've failed to live up to your standards and you are sending me back to Thessalonica anyway? I don't understand. Why? Do you want me to flounder?"

"No," he said sternly, dropping his arm and stepping away. "I want you to stop thinking this journey is about you. Abandon your need to prove yourself capable and be desperate for God's assistance." His voice softened. "I want you to learn to trust God and the indwelling Holy Spirit, Timothy. In the same way that God gives guidance and character, He also gives power.[105] Only the power of the Holy Spirit makes us truly adequate as ministers."[106]

My breathing slowed, and my tension eased. Paul wasn't insulting me. He wanted to assure me that success was not dependent on me, to remind me that I could do all things—but only through Christ who gives me strength.[107]

In the next minutes he shared with me about his own struggles, about how he was learning that God's grace was sufficient for him in spite of them. He told how he had pleaded with the Lord for relief from his eye problems and shortcomings, only to be reassured that God's power reaches its zenith in our lives when we feel the weakest. "So," he finished, "I have learned to boast, not about my strengths and wisdom, but about my frailties, problems, and setbacks—because I know when I am weak, then I am strong."[108]

"You are saying that in our weakness, as we receive the power of God, we are able to build the kingdom of God, for the glory of God," I summarized.

He grinned and slapped me on the back. "Perhaps you are more ready than I realized," he said with a laugh.

For a moment we stood, quiet. Then I asked the question burning my heart. Now that I'd heard Paul's thoughts on my readiness, I began to recognize my own limitations. "How can I make sure I'm leaning on the Lord and not trying to do things in my own power?"

"An excellent question," he smiled, giving my arm a squeeze. "Always remember that the same God who raised Jesus from the dead inhabits you.[109] But it's not enough just to know that; the Lord wants us to depend on Him, like the branch relies on the vine.[110] God is your source of life and strength. Therefore, since everything you need comes from God, you must maintain intimate communion with the Lord. Pray at all times.[111] If you'll do that faithfully, you will lean on Him as your power source."

I bit my lower lip, thinking. "But what if I don't *feel* Him with me?"

"Feelings are unimportant," he shrugged. "What is important is faith. Trust God. When you ask for God's strength, believe God has answered."

Together we walked onward toward the summit where we enjoyed a panoramic view of Athens below and the Aegean Sea off to the southwest. Below us were white rocks, green trees, and red roofs, ending abruptly against the blue expanse of the boat-dotted sea. I could just make out a few islands in the hazy distance. My future suddenly seemed hazy too. Uncertainty made my palms dampen.

I asked Paul to pray for me, and he did. When he concluded his prayer, there in the shadow of the Parthenon, I smiled. Because no matter what lay ahead, I accepted that Christ reigned in me and trusted His Spirit would empower me in a future He could already see. If I'd allow Him to do so, He would continue to work through me.

Whether or not I would continue to let Him remained to be seen.

Grow as a Disciple:

Paul explained to Timothy that the indwelling Holy Spirit provides the power for Christian living. On a typical day, how often do you rely on your strength instead of God's power? Explain your answer. _____

_____

_____

Read Jeremiah 32:17. Is there anything God can't do? ___

_____

_____

Is it better to be confident in yourself or humble before God? Explain. _____

_____

_____

Memory Verse:

Select one of the following verses to commit to memory: 2 Corinthians 4:7 or Ephesians 3:20-21. Write it here for practice. _____

_____

_____

Prepare to Disciple Others:

If a high school senior confided in you about his fear of the future, what encouragement might you give? _____

_____

_____

_____

Chapter 6

DISCOVERING HOPE

A.D. 51

My first solo ministry in Thessalonica went smoothly, much to my relief. I collected data for Paul and answered the Thessalonians' questions about the faith as well as I could. Chief on their list of concerns was the second coming of Christ. When would He appear? What were they supposed to do in the meantime? Thankfully, God empowered me to give good answers and—overall—richly blessed my ministry there. I grew increasingly dependent on Him in those days without the benefit of seeking Paul's wisdom whenever I wanted it. I missed Paul, but I redirected my lonely hours into studying God's Word and better relying on Him.

Several months after I arrived, Silas finished his work in Amphipolis. He stopped by Thessalonica to relay the message that it was time to conclude my ministry there. Together we sailed to Corinth, where we planned to join Paul's efforts. But when Silas and I arrived in Corinth, we discovered that the local Jews were infuriated with our friend's insistence that Jesus was the Messiah. As far as they were concerned, the Messiah had not yet made His appearance. It was no surprise to me at all that their offense made no difference in Paul's determination to keep preaching Jesus as Lord, but I knew the time would come when he would move on. [112]

One night not long after our arrival in Corinth, Paul taught a group of Gentiles in the house of Justus, who lived next to the synagogue[113] Among them was Crispus, the Jewish leader of the synagogue whose rapt attention suggested he was far more open to the gospel message than were his fellow Jews: before the night was over, he and his entire household placed faith in Jesus![114] It proved an encouraging event for all of us.

As Crispus and some of the others lingered after the meeting to ask Paul questions, I slipped outside for a breath of fresh air. I hoped I might run into the beautiful girl who had already disappeared out into the courtyard. I knew Shayna was the daughter of Aquila and Priscilla—also tentmakers like Paul—who were quickly becoming partners in the Corinth ministry. So far, however, I'd had few chances to speak to the young woman. We knew one another's names and had stolen many covert glances and smiles, but I was eager to know her better.

I saw Shayna standing by the fountain just as soon as I stepped over the threshold. The moonlight shimmered over her head covering, and I caught my breath at what a pretty picture she made. "Nice night," I said.

"Most certainly," she said softly, shyly. "You may join me if you like."

I walked over to her, determined to get her to lift her lowered lashes and look me full in the face. I hoped her heart was beating as fast as mine. "Lots of stars tonight," I commented, pointing at the blackness above. "Look, there's Orion."

Shayna raised her face to the sky. Her dark eyes were luminous. "Where? I don't see it."

I pointed out the warrior in the sky, gently resting my hand on her back as I did. I swallowed hard when Shayna nestled closer to me to see where I pointed. Her scent was like a flower garden after a spring rain.

We talked for the next hour, and with each passing moment I grew more enamored with her lovely brown eyes and flashing white smile. I learned she was from Italy, her Jewish-Christian family having fled their villa in Rome when persecution broke out against the believers.

"We hated to leave," she said, "but Claudius evicted all Jews from the city.[115] We had no other choice." Her voice caught. "Timothy, why does the world hate God's people so much?"

I gently took her hand in mine and explained, "Because Satan hates us and he turns the world against us." Paul and my Scripture study had trained me well. "We are God's people and thus the Devil's target," I added soberly. "It's been this way ever since God cursed the serpent."[116]

We spoke a bit longer, our hands still intertwined, until Shayna's father came out and said it was time to go. If he noticed our connection, he didn't speak of it. We were both old enough to marry, though she was several years younger than I, so it could be he anticipated our pairing.

Just before the family left, I found the nerve to ask whether I might call on Shayna the next day. "She knows the area well," I said to her parents, keenly aware of Shayna's eyes on my profile, "and it's so new to me. Perhaps we could go sightseeing? Have a picnic?"

They agreed, so the next morning Shayna and I met just after breakfast and hiked across the Isthmus of Corinth, a narrow strip of land only four miles wide. There Shayna showed me where thousands of slaves pulled ships overland; I was amazed such a thing could be done. To the northwest we could see the Adriatic Sea in the Corinthian Gulf. Then, after crossing the mountain ridge, we were able to look to the southeast and see the Aegean Sea in the Saronic Gulf. On the eastern side we looked down and saw the harbor town of Cencherea: I knew Paul wanted to go there.

When we finally began walking back to Corinth, we stopped to eat. It was breezy on the hilltop, but we found a windbreak beside some large rocks. I was hungry and glad to rest. By that point in the day I'd made up my mind: I still loved to see new places, but I loved Shayna too. One day I wanted her to become my wife and travel partner.

After lunch, I gave Shayna a thin silver bracelet I helped make in the metal shop back in Thessalonica. She seemed impressed and thanked me for the gift. When I gathered a bouquet of daisies for her, she gave a dimpled smile that melted my heart.

Just before we reached the house where she and her family stayed, Shayna asked a question that convinced me she was as in love with me as I was with her. "Do you want a large family, Timothy?"

I smiled slowly and shrugged, choosing my words carefully. "Why not?"

"Big families are important," she, one of six children, said. "The best way to change the world is to raise godly offspring."

I drank in her flawless olive complexion and the beautiful tendrils of dark hair that framed her face. I didn't agree with her reasoning, but I smiled as if I did.

Only a few weeks later the joy of our romance suffered a profound setback when Paul said it was time to leave town. The local Jews had grown so hostile. Paul felt it would be best for us to return to our sponsors in Antioch. I trusted Paul's judgment, but despite the anti-Christian sentiment in Corinth, I hated the thought of leaving Shayna. I considered asking for her hand but knew I'd be rushing things from her parents' point of view.

Thankfully, a short reprieve came when Shayna and her family set sail for Syria with us.[117] I knew we would part soon, but I was determined to make the most out of our last few days together. I liked the sea, and I would carry the euphoria of sailing with Shayna for years. The ocean spray made her hair glisten in the sunshine, and we shared many laughs.

After we made port in Ephesus, Aquila let us know that he and his family would disembark there. I guess he waited to announce his plans because by then he knew how much I hated to be separated from his daughter. Though I'm sure he intended it as a kindness, I felt heartbroken by the abrupt good-bye. Shayna had made no promises, leaving me to wonder as she made her way to shore, *Will she wait for a traveler like me? Or will she choose another mate, someone content to stay in one place?* I had no right to ask her those questions. We'd known one another for mere months, and I couldn't say with any assurance that I'd see her again.

"Take heart," Paul said from behind me as I stood waving at the departing family from my place aboard deck. "We might return to Ephesus someday." He patted my back. "Lord willing."[118]

When our ship sailed away, we navigated eastward across the Great Sea toward Caesarea. Feeling dejected, I watched the clouds as the others considerately gave me space. Sometimes the fluffy white shapes in the sky reminded me of Shayna. In spite of myself, I dreamed not of the adventures ahead but of one day reuniting with the girl who had so thoroughly captured my heart.

Nineteen days later we made port near the city of Joppa, the place from which Jonah had sailed when running from the Lord.[119] By that time, I no longer thought of cities as places of endless excitement: I knew many were full of evils best left unspoken. They certainly were not the ports of happiness and fulfillment I'd once assumed. Still, cities have their charms; each has its own personality. Jerusalem, I'd been told as we drew near it, was a city I'd never forget.

The Holy City, nestled in the Judean Mountains between the Great Sea and the Dead Sea, was four thousand years old. The locale so prominent in the stories of Scripture was first under the control of the Jebusites before being captured by David. He'd turned it into the mountain stronghold from which he ruled during the days when Israel was a united kingdom. His son Solomon later built the temple there, though both the city and that temple ultimately were destroyed by the Babylonians. Thankfully, Cyrus the Great later allowed the Jews who had been exiled from Jerusalem to return, rebuild, and reoccupy the area. Though in time the land fell under Roman occupation, the place was still important to the Jewish people. Christians, too, loved Jerusalem: it was there that Jesus visited as a young boy, ministered, and ultimately died as a sacrificial Lamb. Death could not hold Jesus, however: He rose again three days after dying. And it was from Jerusalem that His first followers multiplied and scattered, working to take His truth to the ends of the world.

I thought about Jerusalem's history a lot as we approached. The city center—Herod's temple where Jesus had taught—sat on a hill, clearly visible long before we reached the city gates.

"Before we go inside," I said to Paul, "would you take me to Golgotha?"

He nodded once, seeming to understand that I wanted to see the place where the Lord gave His life. It went without saying that I'd want to pass by the tomb He'd vacated as well. (We would not enter it; new occupants now rested inside.) Paul, Silas, and I skirted the city walls until we came to a dirt road leading up to a rocky hill.

I knew as soon as I saw the place that I'd remember it for the rest of my life. Some say Golgotha looks like a human skull, the rocks and crevices comprising the hill giving that impression. I agreed with what I'd heard: when I blurred my vision, I could see why it had been given that nickname. It was more than a little creepy. As we neared the spot, I noticed that the chatter of other travelers around us had stalled when the eerie sight came into view. All lightheartedness stopped. Only whispering seemed appropriate at the place where so many people had been gruesomely executed.

"You go ahead," Silas said, stepping off the path. "I've been up there before." I might've imagined it, but I think I saw him shiver.

Alongside Paul I continued up a narrow trail that circled around the hill, leading to the top. The steep walkway, probably once a goat trail, was no wider than my shoulders. It was slippery because of all the loose gravel, and I found myself wondering how anyone could carry a cross up it. The thought of the Lord stumbling His way to the top on my behalf raised the hair on the back of my neck. What love He had for me!

I soon found that the top of the rock formation was level. Jerusalem—the city over which Christ had wept—was clearly visible from that vantage point. A quick survey of the place revealed several scattered holes cut into the rock; I knew without being told that they'd been added to hold crosses upright. A few pieces of splintered wood and one rusty spike half buried in the dust were the only other clues to the spot's significance.

This, I knew, was holy ground. Though long swept away by time and wind, Christ's blood had flowed here, draining into the gravel on which I stood. This was the place where God demonstrated His love for humanity by pouring out His wrath toward sin on His Son. This was where God purchased my salvation. In spite of myself, a hot tear burned down my cheek and into my beard. I was still trying not to weep with gratitude when we passed the place where His body once lay.

After only a brief stay in Jerusalem, Paul led us onward to Antioch Syria and beyond, largely with the goal of revisiting the churches earlier planted.[120] It didn't take me long to realize that our route would soon take us to Lystra, to the home and family I had not seen in four long years.

Just before we reached my town, Paul made one last stop in Derbe. We were so close to Lystra I would have preferred to keep going. But Paul wanted to make sure the believers there were faring well. Sadly, however, we found no trace of the church that budded under the teaching of Paul and Barnabas. If some believers still lived in Derbe, we couldn't find them. A brief investigation explained why: Nicolas DoM and the Judaizers had set up shop there not long ago, slowly infecting the church with the idea that they must adhere to impossible rules and regulations. In time, such lies led to the death of the local church body: believers either moved, returned to Judaism, or turned to the less demanding idols of their culture. Paul was furious.

By the time we moved on from Derbe, I was more than ready for a happy reunion. But that's not what I found. My mother began to cry before I even had a chance to greet her. "I'm so sorry," she said, "but Grandma passed away last year. Oh, Timothy! She was so proud of you. She prayed for you every day! She tried to guess where you might be. I know she hated to leave without seeing you again."

News of Grandma's death stunned me. I felt crushed. Angry.

Grieved. I wanted to break down and weep, but I never found the right time. Besides, Paul and Silas were quick to comfort me every chance they could.

Silas suggested fishing competitions between the two of us, never expecting me to talk about my feelings but simply providing distraction and a comforting presence. That was his way. Paul was quick to teach me how to remember my Grandmother Lois by her faith, to remind me that our parting was not final, and to use my sadness as an opportunity to help me learn to anticipate heaven.

Though similar conversations would follow, the one Paul and I had about a week after I learned Grandma was gone would stick with me for years.

"Again, I am so sorry, Son," he began. "Death is a cruel enemy. But thank God it is swallowed up in victory through our Lord. Though Adam's sin ensured death would come to all, Jesus—the second Adam— came to give us life. This is not the end for your grandmother Lois."

I mumbled my thanks, having every intention of walking away from the conversation. But Paul stopped me. He grabbed my elbow gently and motioned for me to follow him.

Moments later we were inside my house where Paul slept and stored tent-making supplies. I watched for a moment as he dug through his things before finally settling on one item and handing it to me. Clearly he wanted me to examine it.

"Do you know what this is?" he asked, his eyes kind.

I held it up to the window's light. "Is it wool?"

"No," he answered. "This is *cilicium*. It comes from Cilicia and is made from woven goat hair. Where I grew up in Tarsus, my family ran a textile business. We used to buy and sell *cilicium*. Of all the materials on the market, this is the best. People use it not only for tents, but even in camel saddles."

"Is it expensive?" I asked, more interested in being polite to my mentor than in trying to figure out where he intended to go with this little lesson.

"Yes, very. It's durable, pliable, and highly prized. Yet even *cilicium* wears out. The expensive tent made with it today will be a thing for the rag pile in time." He smiled gently, eyes sad.

I handed him the fabric. He took it and asked me to sit down with him on the floor. I agreed.

"Timothy, in many ways our human bodies are mere tents. When we are young, our bodies are new and strong, but time wears them down. Sooner or later, even the best tents become tattered and unravel. We can't count on them as we once did. We begin looking forward to the day when we can exchange the old for the new."

I thought for a moment. "You are saying Grandma's 'tent' wore out," I said.

He nodded. "Because of the curse of sin on this fallen world, this life is temporary. But when we lay these earthly tents aside in death, God gives us eternal buildings in their place.[121] Moreover, those new bodies will enjoy a new home in heaven, a place prepared by the Lord Himself."

I smiled in spite of my sadness. Paul's excitement was catching. "When Jesus lived on this earth," he said, "He worked as a carpenter.[122] Now I am sure He did quality craftsmanship as I cannot imagine our Lord doing shoddy work, can you?"

I shook my head.

"The Lord told His disciples He was going to prepare new homes for them in heaven.[123] New homes for all His followers!" He stood and began pacing. Then he drew to an abrupt stop right in front of me. "He's been up in heaven for close to twenty years now, Timothy. Don't you imagine He's done some beautiful work for us?"

I nearly laughed at his enthusiasm, at the thought of Grandma inviting the risen Lord into her heavenly house for a meal. "Thank you, Paul," I said. "You have renewed my hope."

He seemed blessed by the news. I smiled too, pleased by the chance to give back to the man who had so radically influenced my life. "So what do you think we will do when we get to heaven?" I asked, choosing a light tone meant to signal I was feeling better.

"We will walk with Jesus," He said, as if he could think of nothing greater. "And we will worship Him. And we will learn from Him. And we will have the chance to enjoy His creation as it was meant to be: death a lie, tears forgotten, each day filled with joy and peace."

"And you feel we'll see one another there?"

"Of course," he said. "I *know* there will be fellowship. The Lord Himself said saints will gather from the east and west and sit down with Abraham, Isaac, and Jacob in the kingdom of heaven."[124] He rubbed his hands together and chuckled. "Just think of it! You and me and Silas and the others, dining with the patriarchs of old!"

"You really think we will recognize one another in heaven? I mean, we've never met those men. And surely the Lord wouldn't leave Grandma as a badly bent elder leaning on a cane in heaven, would He?"

"Of course not," Paul said with a twinkle in his eyes. "I predict she'll run to meet you when you get there—probably more a girl than the aged woman you always knew. Yes, we will know one another." He paused, thinking. "You know, Peter once told me he recognized Moses and Elijah when they appeared before Jesus up on the mountain.[125] I don't know how he knew those men on sight—they'd been dead for hundreds of years—but he did know them. It makes one wonder whether we'll have some new sense of recognition when we get to heaven, a new level of knowledge or insight we can't quite imagine today."

We spoke for several minutes more, Paul's descriptions of heaven inspiring hope within me. In fact, I realized, that was just what Paul spent his life doing: he pointed people to the hope of Jesus every chance he could.

That same week I announced an important decision to Mother and Hitty. I would not return to farming; I wanted to follow in Paul's steps, to spend my life as one who offered hope. If there was one thing I wanted to be, it was a man of God like my father in the Lord, Paul the apostle.

Though Hitty complained about me "shirking my responsibility to the family," she was forced to shut her mouth when I produced a bag of my earnings from work as a smith. With our uncle's help, the farm was flourishing, and the money I'd provided would keep them well for some time. Besides, Mother had confided in me that Hitty had gained the interest of a certain man in Lystra. Undoubtedly, they'd soon marry and Hitty and Mother would live under his care.

Mother affirmed my choice with a tearful smile and gave me her blessing. I hated to leave Mother again, but God's call weighed heavily on my heart. The recent experience with grief had only underscored the importance of my evangelistic ministry. I felt a responsibility to share the gospel with as many people as possible so they too could find hope through Jesus Christ.

I sensed a strange mixture of sorrow and gladness as I packed my bag to head back out again with Paul. I'd left Lystra the first time as a boy. Now I was a man of twenty. Previously, I was self-consumed, thinking only of me. Now with greater maturity, I focused my attention upon Christ and concerned myself with the needs of others.

As Lystra disappeared from view, I wondered, *How much more might I change before my next return home?*

Grow as a Disciple:

The passing of Timothy's grandmother Lois became an opportunity for him to reflect on life after death. For you, is heaven a probability or a certainty? _____

_____

List at least five people you hope to meet in heaven. _____

_____

_____

Read Revelation 21—22 and make a list of what will be in heaven and another list of what won't be in heaven.

_____

_____

_____

_____

Memory Verse:

Commit either John 14:1-2 or 1 John 5:13 to memory. Write it here for practice. _____

_____

_____

Prepare to Disciple Others:

If you were asked to speak at the funeral of a Christian friend, what encouraging truths about heaven might you share? _____

_____

_____

_____

Before proceeding to Part Two of Timothy's story,
please visit *mitchmartin.org/ resources*
and watch the PowerPoint titled

"Identification with Christ."

**From this point forward, the focus of the narrative
will shift to what it means to be "in Christ."**

PART TWO

From Paul, your fellow servant of Christ Jesus.

To Timothy, my faithful son.

> *Until I come, Timothy, devote yourself to the public reading of Scripture, to exhortation, to teaching. Do not neglect the gift you have, which was given you by prophecy when the council of elders laid their hands on you. Practice these things, immerse yourself in them, so that all may see your progress. Keep a close watch on yourself and on the teaching. Persist in this, for by so doing you will save both yourself and your hearers.*

— 1 TIMOTHY 4:13-16, author paraphrase

Chapter 7

DISCOVERING
CHRIST'S AUTHORITY

A.D. 53

My second trip with Paul and Silas started better than the first. We did not encounter bandits, and both my attitude and focus were much improved compared to how I began my first journey.

Together we trekked west over the mountains, following the Sebastian Way. When we finally made it down the other side of the pass, I found my steps quickening. We were about to enter the great city of Ephesus, the place where I'd last seen Shayna.

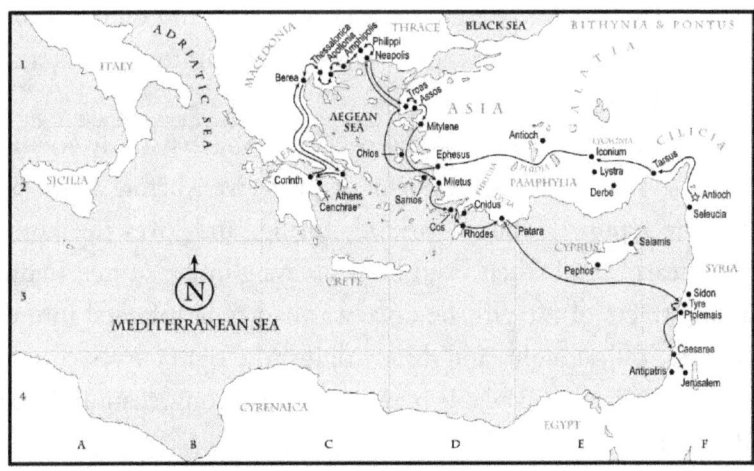

Ephesus is the capital of the Roman province of Asia. It is located in western Asia Minor at the mouth of the Cayster River and serves as an important seaport and a bustling commercial center. The city boasts a population of a quarter of a million and has the distinction of being the third largest city in the Roman Empire.

Paul warned us as we approached Ephesus that we might find danger there. The city was prosperous, its citizens hungry for entertainment. They enjoyed watching gladiatorial matches at the city's massive 25,000-seat theater, and they were deeply devoted to the goddess Artemis. In fact, much of the economic vitality of Ephesus arises from arriving pilgrims worshiping at her impressive temple.

The Temple of Artemis, four times larger than the Parthenon, is considered one of the Seven Wonders of the World. Rumor has it that a gigantic statue of Artemis, the alleged protector of young women, sits inside the place—though I would never approach the building closely enough to find out for myself. The idol's throne, we heard, is directly behind a mysterious rock said to have fallen from heaven.[126] When I first heard of it, I doubted the story. In time, however, I'd learn that similar stones did indeed fall from the sky.

Soon after we arrived in Ephesus, Paul was able to reconnect with Aquila and Priscilla, who had become pillars in the local church. The pair had proven solid in their commitment to Christ, always eager to lead people to Him with sound theology and ongoing discipleship efforts. They led a Bible study in their house,[127] and on occasion, they even trained itinerant preachers[128]—a valuable gift to the greater church body as a whole.

It didn't take me long to discover that Shayna still lived with her parents, available and as beautiful as ever. Even before I saw her, I'd heard the reports: "Shayna is kind, caring, and loves the Lord with all her heart." And when I did first catch a glimpse of her, I admitted that any traces of the girl she once was had only softened into deeper loveliness. Tall, straight, and thin with just the right curves, Shayna was dazzling. And every available man in the local congregation, it seemed, had noticed.

I wanted my relationship with Shayna to resume as before, but Shayna treated me with a distant politeness that made me wonder whether I'd only dreamed our attraction of the previous year. It didn't take me long to see she led a busy life surrounded by countless admirers, and while I couldn't discern which of the men flocking around her was her favorite, I knew the title was no longer mine—if it ever had been.

Disappointed, I chose to lose myself in busyness. I got a job with the local smith, working mornings and nights when I was needed. In the afternoons I helped Paul teach new Christians at the school of Tyrannus.[129] In the morning hours the school was devoted to teaching students to dominate one another through persuasive speech and rhetoric. Paul used it to share about Christ's humility and sacrificial love—a contrast that raised some eyebrows. I saw Shayna at worship on Sundays, briefly and from afar, but I did not pursue her.

My profession as a smith progressed quickly when the master craftsman's son became temporarily disabled because of an accident. Almost immediately, I advanced from running the smelting furnace to actually forging the metal. I fiercely pounded orange pieces of molten iron into submission, using secrets as old as Tubal-Cain.[130] Due to God's blessings, I soon demonstrated a knack for metalworking, and my reputation spread. The shop owner earned good money selling the knives and swords I fashioned, and he generously shared the profits with me.

Every day on my walk to work, I passed numerous beggars. On one particular morning I thought my heart would break at the sight of a very young mother tending her babies—twins—while also begging for handouts. I stopped and gave her a few coins, deciding that I'd look for her each day. By the end of the week, I had introduced her to Christ. And, praise the Lord, that Sunday she and her babies were adopted into one of our believing households. Whatever circumstances had led her to that point in her life, she was no longer an unwed mother raising fatherless girls. She was a daughter of King Jesus, forgiven and set free. Both she and her children were welcomed into our church body as long-lost daughters.

Other similar connections were made during my time in Ephesus, but much of my focus had to be directed into my work. One day, just after I'd made it to the forge, I was approached by a man carrying a bag. Inside it, he said, were rocks and an elephant tusk. When he claimed the rocks were thrown to earth from Jupiter, the king of the gods, my interest piqued. I cared nothing for pagan stories, but if the stones had fallen from heaven as he suggested, they were likely rich in metal. Smiths knew much about these prized chunks from the sky, smaller versions of the one said to be in the Temple of Artemis. Blades forged from the metal within them stayed sharper longer. They were highly prized.

The man asked me to use the metallic rocks to make two ivory-handled daggers, incorporating the contents of the bag. "One is for me," he said, "and it should be the finest. But the other," he smiled widely, "is payment for you."

My overseer, the shop owner, stepped up to negotiate with the customer, arguing that he should be able to keep the remaining rocks and ivory for the use of his fire and the redirection of my time. The man placed his bag in my hands and shrugged. "What do I need with rocks and bones? It's the knife I want."

The shop owner, I knew, had made quite the deal. Eager to get to work, I agreed to do my part in fulfilling the man's order promptly. "Both blades will be fine indeed," I told the unusual customer. "You may select the one you prefer."

Upon completion, those exquisite daggers became my masterpieces. The customer was overjoyed with his. I began to carry my own knife from heaven in a leather scabbard strapped to my right hip. Given all the odd pagan sights and dangers in the huge city, I was glad to have a concealed weapon at the ready.

One afternoon on my way home, I witnessed an unforgettable scene. Running down the road toward me in a panic were seven naked men, bloody and screaming.[131] I shook my head in disgust at the display, moved toward the side of the road along with the other bystanders, and looked down as they passed. Who knew what had led them to such a public show of depravity? Had they no more decency than to expose themselves and then demand the crowd's attention? There were children in the streets!

I startled when a man standing beside me nudged me in the ribs. "That'll teach those seven sons of Sceva, eh?" he cackled, breathless and watching the men race by us as if delighting in a good joke.

"You know them?" I asked.

He looked at me and apologized. He'd thought I was his grown son, whom he'd assumed was right behind him.

I asked what he meant about the runners getting taught a lesson, and he told me a local demon-possessed man had roughed up the seven men after they attempted to exorcise the devil that tormented him. "I was there, my boy and I, standing in the crowd to see what would happen," he explained. "They've been walking around this area for weeks, acting like no one's holier than them and giving the impression they've got all the answers," he scoffed. "When they called a public meeting to prove it, I thought we'd go and see if there was anything to it. Maybe they'd say some fancy words and they'd do a miracle. I thought it might be entertaining."

I wasn't surprised he'd thought a miracle might take place. The Lord had been doing some amazing work through His followers in Ephesus. Surely word was getting around.

"And what happened?" I asked.

He sneered at the memory of it. "Those pretenders don't have any power. When all their chanting and nonsense failed, they called on the Jesus that Paul fellow preaches," he spat.

I tensed at his venom and the mention of my friend's name. Paul was growing increasingly known in Ephesus lately, largely because the Lord had been working through him to accomplish healings comparable with those Christ had displayed. Clearly the Holy Spirit was working through Paul to draw the Ephesians to Jesus.[132]

"And then?" I pressed, heart racing.

"Then the possessed man went wild," he reported, gesturing with his hands and crossing his eyes to illustrate.

I backed up a step, surprised.

"I tell you, I ran for my life when things started to go awry," the man continued. "All this time those seven have been making a show of what good Jews they are, but when it comes time to put the exorcism skills they claim to have to the test, they go calling on the power of men they claim to reject. Stupidest thing I've ever heard of! Were I a spirit, I'd have whipped them too!"

A shiver of terror went up my spine. The hairs on the back of my neck bristled. These men—believers or not—had called on the name of Jesus and had been stripped and beaten by a demon in spite of the Name? I was appalled. Why hadn't Christ silenced the unclean spirit?

Later that afternoon I asked Paul to join me for a walk up in the hills outside the city, on the pretense that I wanted to watch the sunset over the harbor. From our elevated vantage point, we enjoyed a view of Ephesus below. Soon I began to share my anxiety and questions about the botched exorcism, uncertain what had gone wrong.

Paul stopped by a large Cyprus tree and asked for my knife. Then he proceeded to cut two jagged circles into its bark. Following the grain of the wood, he scratched a line connecting the two circles. "Do you remember this?"

"Yes, sir," I nodded. "I remember this diagram about how Christ came down to us."

He smiled. "Good," he said. "Now this time, I want you to see how this line showing that Christ came down to us also goes up?"

I nodded once.

"This fact signifies that Christ ascended into heaven at the completion of His ministry and today is at the Father's right hand. But it also serves to remind you, as a Christ-follower, of where you belong."

"Alright," I said. "I'm listening."

"At the moment of our salvation, the Father baptized us into Christ,"[133] Paul taught, his voice still as rich and powerful as when I'd first met him. "This means we were placed into Christ and share in His death and resurrection.[134] When the Lord arose from the dead, we also were raised with Him. And when the Lord ascended into heaven, we went along in a sense—because we are in Christ."[135]

"But I'm physically here," I retorted good naturedly.

He grinned and slapped my shoulder affectionately. "I know this is an abstract concept," he answered, "but concentrate. Bodily you are here on earth, but spiritually speaking, you are positioned with Christ in heaven, at the Father's right hand."[136]

"I'm in Christ," I agreed, seeing his point. "Though my body is here on earth, in spirit I am seated at the Father's right hand."

"Good. Now what is the significance of sitting at the king's right hand?"

"The right hand designates honor," I replied.

"Correct," he enthused, eyes sparkling, their corners heavily creased. "So, since you are in Christ, seated at the right hand of the Father, you enjoy royal privileges."

"You are saying those who belong to the Father through faith in Jesus are special."

"Indeed." He leaned against the carvings he'd made on the tree, his expression thoughtful and his arms crossed. Then, in the next several moments he explained how his authority to heal or to drive out unclean spirits had nothing to do with him; instead, that authority had everything to do with Christ. "The Devil is not afraid of you or me," he insisted, "but he *trembles* before Jesus. And you and I rest in Christ."

"I think I understand," I said. "The seven sons of Sceva were unwise because they tried to take on Satan in their own power. They thought they could use the name of Jesus like a good luck charm."

Paul nodded and continued. "Spiritual warfare—that is fighting against the Devil's evil with the light of God's truth—can only be done from our position in Christ. When Christ arose from the dead, the Father lifted Him up to glory. He invited Him to sit far above all principalities, powers, and spiritual forces of darkness.[137] The Lord Jesus now has all things under His feet."[138]

Paul stood up straight. "And since we are in Christ through faith, that means we too are far above the enemy, Satan. He is under our feet, and this means we fight from victory, not for victory."

Paul invited me to climb higher up the hill with him, hiking alongside me in silence for a long while before we sat down to catch our breath. "Do you see the golden eagle there?" Paul pointed out over the valley.

I said I did. The raptor glided in high, broad circles just in front of our resting spot. Even from a distance, I could see his wingspan was massive—at least eight feet across. Likely he was hunting a rabbit or a bird, though they were known to occasionally take down larger animals such as deer and wolves.

"Do you know why golden eagles are such skilled hunters?" Paul asked.

"I believe it is because they have extraordinary vision and powerful talons."

"And," he added, "they attack from above and swoop down on their unsuspecting prey. That suggests position makes the difference." Paul watched the bird, careful to keep his bad eye shut as he did so. "The same is true in spiritual warfare, Timothy. We prevail in our fight against Satan because we are above him in Christ."

A passage from the prophet Isaiah came to mind, *Those who wait on the LORD shall renew their strength; They shall mount up with wings like eagles.*[139] I wondered if Paul was thinking of the verse but chose not to interrupt.

"We must remember," Paul taught, turning to look at me and opening his eye as he did, "that Jesus is stronger than angels.[140] This is important to remember—especially since the Devil is nothing but a fallen angel.[141] Satan has no power, then, other than what the Lord allows. He is not the equal opposite of Christ. He is inferior in every way. Only the Lord is in complete control. And you and I can call on His authority over evil."

I thought about that, weighing it against the report I'd heard earlier. "But what if I am ever in combat against Satan and he doesn't obey me?" I asked.

"We are not in a physical fistfight with Satan," he said. "We are in an invisible war against the spiritual forces of darkness.[142] But if you minister to someone tormented by an evil spirit or only sense the presence of darkness, you can know you have authority over evil because of your union with Christ. If the demon refuses to obey when you reject him in the name of Jesus, then you must trust God and stand firm.[143] You may need to fast and pray,[144] but the Lord promised those who believe would cast out demons.[145] We are not to live in fear of them."

"So all I have to do is trust God and stand up against the Devil?"

"Yes. Think of the nature of authority over darkness being a bit like a mother's authority over her defiant toddler. There may be moments when the two stand off in a battle of wills. The mother may have to repeat herself and insist on her way, but if she will not waiver, the child will obey eventually. He has no real choice: her power far exceeds his because of her position in the natural hierarchy. Much the same is true in spiritual warfare."

The parenting analogy drummed up long-forgotten memories of my father, his voice raging as he insulted me over small infractions. With it came thoughts of a new believer who'd been joining our fellowship meals lately. I'd heard rumors that in his work as a fisherman he was known to talk to the air as if the Devil were an unseen villain toying with his day. "You slimy old snake," he would rage at Satan in instances where he missed his daily quota, snagged his net, or met with some other calamity. It sounded as if he expended far more energy on fighting the enemy with words than he spent in prayer to God. I mentioned the matter to Paul, and he sighed. He knew of whom I spoke.

"We mustn't look for a demon behind every tree," he said. "Our thoughts should be on things above. But to answer your questions, casting out demons is not accomplished by religious rituals or by the volume of your voice. And it certainly doesn't help to go around insulting the enemy as if he were a sparring partner—even the archangel Michael did not insult the Devil but called on the Lord to rebuke him.[146] Instead, we should know our identity in Christ. And, no matter what evil we encounter, we must abide in Him."

Later that same week, I got an opportunity to put Paul's teaching into action. While running errands one afternoon, I cut through the temple district. I admired the immensity and beauty of the complex, but the activity in and around the pagan places of worship gave me the creeps. I knew that the sacrifices offered in that district were not made to God but to demons,[147] servants of Satan who loved the worship of Artemis and other worthless idols because they took devotion away from God.

Suddenly, I felt out of place. I walked faster. The air was heavy with a presence I'd never taken the time to notice before.

I winced, tightened my fists, and then swallowed. I mentally checked to see whether I carried my dagger. The desire to run was great.

But then I remembered what Paul told me about Christ's authority. "Get behind me, Satan," I whispered as I walked past flocks of lost people looking for a connection with heaven in all the wrong places. "I belong to Jesus Christ, my Savior and Redeemer." I exhaled, feeling some of the darkness dissipate. 'I am in Him. And you are under our feet.' "

Little did I know that I would cling hard to those words in the coming months. Storm clouds were brewing on the horizon of my life. Dark days would soon try my soul.

Grow as a Disciple:

Please visit *mitchmartin.org/resources* and
watch the PowerPoint titled

"Spiritual Authority."

Just as Timothy initially trusted in his dagger, people rely
on many forms of physical protection. On what do you rely
to keep you and your family safe? _____

_____

_____

Finish this sentence: The believer's identification with
Christ is the source of his authority over _____.
Explain what that has to do with fighting not for victory,
but from victory. _____

_____

_____

Psalm 8 describes the hierarchy of creation. Read the
passage and then rank the following in order of power and
importance:

    ___Animals

    ___Angels

    ___God

    ___Man

Is Satan equal to God? Explain. _____

_____

_____

Memory Verse:

Select and memorize either Romans 16:20 or Ephesians 6:10. Write here for practice. _____

_____

_____

_____

Prepare to Disciple Others:

Read Ephesians 6:10-18. Pretend a new believer has approached you, concerned that he won't be able to stand firm in his faith but will quickly fall back into his old sinful habits. How might you use this passage to encourage him?

_____

_____

_____

_____

_____

_____

_____

_____

_____

Chapter 8

DISCOVERING SERENITY

A.D. 56

The Lord blessed our three years in Ephesus, causing the gospel to advance like a tidal wave in all directions. Everyone in Asia had heard the word of the Lord Jesus,[148] and Paul felt we were running out of new places to reach.[149] It was time to move on.

I knew Paul had long wanted us to go see Rome, the biggest and most influential city in the world. But first, he announced we needed to return to Jerusalem for Pentecost.[150] (Pentecost marked the morning when the Holy Spirit first fell on the disciples after the Lord's ascension.) Paul arranged for a quick tour through Macedonia and Achaia on our way there.[151]

As we prepared to sail for Jerusalem, I wondered why my relationship with Shayna had stalled three years ago, never progressing past friendship in the many months both she and I lived and served in Ephesus. My only consolation was that she'd never promised herself to another man. For all I knew she'd chosen to remain single in order to focus her energies on doing the Lord's work. As much as I hated to admit it, I'd not gotten over her. I wasn't sure I ever would.

The church leaders from Ephesus met our ship at the port of Miletus,[152] eager for one last visit with Paul before we sailed beyond their reach. Paul spoke words of encouragement to them[153] while Silas and I stood at his side, but I don't remember much about the meeting because, right before Paul began, Aquila handed me a note. It felt as if it burned my hand when he told me it was from Shayna.

As soon as the meeting dispersed, I boarded the ship and quickly removed the seal from my missive. I couldn't read it fast enough.

> *From Shayna, daughter of Aquila*
>
> *To Timothy, honored by God*
>
> *How I sincerely regret we were not able to spend more time together when you were in Ephesus. After you left, I realized just how much I continue to care for you. I so respect the servant of our Lord you have become.*
>
> *Timothy, I will pray for you and the other missionaries every day, for your safety and good health. Please be careful. I miss you.*
>
> *Write me soon.*

I read and reread the letter once our journey was underway, both pleased and confused by it. Weeks ago I had asked Shayna to correspond with me during our travels only to receive a disappointing comment about how she expected she would be too busy to write. Now, much to my surprise, it seemed she had not only found the time for me but had remembered the affection we'd once shared. The girl made me crazy, and in spite of my aggravation, I found myself contemplating a long, tough swim back to Ephesus.

"What you looking for, boy?" asked a sailor to my right as I scanned the distant shoreline.

I turned to him, noticing his gray hair, wrinkled face, and bare feet. "I was just looking to see if I could spot my girl."

"A bit far out now for that, lad," he chuckled.

"It doesn't matter. I'm not sure I understand her anyway," I said to myself, not realizing I'd spoken aloud.

The sailor laughed loudly. "Oh lad, no one knows the way of a woman. Why, she's a mystery, just the way the gods made her." He playfully punched my upper arm. "Don't try to figure her out, man. Just love her, and return to her as soon as you can."

I studied the old salt, absorbing his wisdom. I wondered whether he had a sweetheart waiting for him on some distant shore.

"A woman is like the weather, my boy," he said just before he got back to work. "You can never really know what she'll do." He gave an exaggerated wink. "But that's part of the fun."

I slipped Shayna's letter into a fold of my robe as I watched the sailor head back to his duties. A heated discussion between Paul and Silas drew my attention. Silas was pleading with our leader about something, likely making one last request that he rethink our destination. Numerous people had cautioned Paul against going to Jerusalem, but Paul ignored their warnings and proceeded anyway.[154] He was fully convinced it was to that great city we should go.

With every passing day we drew closer to Jerusalem, finally arriving in Caesarea where we lodged with Philip the Evangelist. He was one of the original seven deacons in the Jerusalem church[155] and an effective revival preacher[156] and soul-winner.[157] Our team felt an immediate connection with Philip and appreciated his family's gracious Christian hospitality.[158] I was not prepared, however, for the overt interest of his daughter, Bayla.

Philip's two-story house held animals on the first level and people on the second. It had a flattop roof. When we first entered Philip's dwelling, his four daughters welcomed us by washing the dust from our feet. Of the four, Bayla was the second from the oldest and most beautiful. She was breathtaking, wide smiled and well curved. I grinned like a fool when the voluptuous girl knelt before me to wash my feet. When she boldly met my eyes as she did so, the room started to feel warm and my mouth went dry.

Throughout the evening as we spoke at length with Philip, Bayla found reasons to brush against me, staring at me the way I'd often stared at Shayna. The realization made me uncomfortable, and I determined not to give the girl encouragement. Still, her actions were tantalizing.

Philip told us all about Caesarea-by-the-Sea, a beautiful city with a handsome man-made port. Built by Herod the Great in honor of Caesar Augustus, Caesarea served as the capital of the province of Judea. It was from this location that Pontius Pilate—the man who had ultimately handed Christ over for crucifixion—governed Judea for ten years. Caesarea was also the place where Simon Peter shared the gospel with the Gentile Cornelius, leading him to faith in the Lord.[159] Both Pilate and Cornelius left legacies, but they could not have been more different.

Paul asked Philip about his fellow deacon Nicolas DoM, the man who had only continued to be a plague on the church throughout our ministry in Ephesus. "When did he go so wrong?"

"Nicolas is an innately spiritual man," Philip said. "Unfortunately, in his relentless quest for truth, he has left himself open to error. It pains me to say this—there was a time when I considered him a brother—but I've come to think he's unstable. In fact, I'm not sure he was truly ever a Christian."

"Well, he sure has been a pain in our sides," I commented. "Seems like he follows us everywhere and…"

Paul sent me a glance that said I was wandering into the waters of gossip. He summed up the situation. "The trouble is Nicolas DoM's pretty convincing, even if he is wrong. We are going to have to work harder than ever to protect the new believers. They must learn God's truth so they can better identify the enemy's lies."

The second night of our stay, a mysterious visitor came to Philip's house. The prophet Agabus was an intelligent, probably educated, man in rough, tattered clothing. After supper, he asked Paul to remove his belt. When he went along with the odd request, Agabus waved the belt in the air for all to see before sitting on the ground in front of our leader. Then he tied his feet and hands with the belt and made this shocking pronouncement: "Thus says the Holy Spirit, 'So shall the

Jews at Jerusalem bind the man who owns this belt, and deliver him into the hands of the Gentiles.'"[160]

Someone—perhaps Philip's wife—gasped at the words before the room grew quiet. Remarkably, the Lord had sent a prophet into our midst who carried a dire warning. Should Paul continue on to Jerusalem, he would face capture by the Jews. Worse, it sounded as if he might end up standing before the Roman courts, perhaps pleading for his life.

All at once everyone in the room started talking, urging Paul to rethink his plans. But he finally shouted for our attention and said, "I don't care if they throw me in prison or take my life. I must testify about Jesus."[161]

Silas and I, plus Philip and his family, reasoned with Paul[162] for the next hour—long after Agabus departed. But like a stone wall, the apostle would not budge. Finally, I watched in disbelief when the others surrendered and said, "The will of the Lord be done."[163] For once, I wasn't certain whether Paul was following God's will or his own stubborn need to advance his personal mission. After all, the Lord had sent a warning.

When things settled down, I asked Paul to go up to our rooftop sleeping quarters with me. He put down his half-eaten pomegranate and wiped the red juice from his chin whiskers. Then I followed him up the ladder, leaving our friends behind while we stepped into the fresh air where we could hear the surf of the Great Sea in the distance.

It would soon be bedtime, so almost immediately, I confronted Paul. "You've made your point. You're brave enough to go to Jerusalem. No one questions that. So please, Paul. Please don't walk into a trap. The Lord sent you a warning for a reason."

Surprise followed by disappointment creased my friend's face. "Oh, Timothy. Of all the people who should understand this, I thought you would."

I hated to see him unhappy with me, but I despised the thought of the church losing such a fine leader should he fall into trouble as Agabus pronounced. I clenched my fists and tried not to shout. "Well,

I'm sorry, Paul. But I just don't understand you choosing to throw your life away! Jerusalem is too dangerous now. You should reconsider."

A moment passed, then several. Judging by his silence and the expression in his eyes, I could see I was getting nowhere, so I changed tactics. "Let's travel straight to Spain instead. It's probably safer, and the people there need to hear about Jesus too."

Paul sighed, smiled. "Come, sit down with me, Timothy." He sat on the ledge of the roof, careful not to crush the little red peppers the family had drying there.

I sat, feeling my anger die down almost immediately. I'd come a long way in the last several years. "I'm sorry," I said, tempted to plead with him to avoid Jerusalem if only for the sake of my feelings. "Whatever you have to say, I'll listen."

"Do you remember what we talked about back in Ephesus, when I scratched a carving into the tree?" Paul asked.

"Sure, I remember. You said I am in Christ, seated at the right hand of the Father."

"Good. Now listen, Timothy. This means you participate in *both* His life and death.[164] Just as you reign with Christ on His throne, so also you die with Christ on His cross. You and I have been crucified with Christ.[165] And that, my dear friend, is why I must go to Jerusalem."

I puzzled over his words for a moment, ignoring the new concerns they raised: Paul, too, could end up on a cross should he continue with his plans. "But Paul, Jesus died over twenty-five years ago. How can you claim we're crucified with Him? I don't understand."

"God is eternal," he said. "He exists before, above, and beyond time. So although Christ's crucifixion occurred in the dimension of time, it also took place in the larger realm of eternity. Our salvation experience is an eternal event. Thus, when we say we are united with Christ on the cross, we acknowledge our participation in an event outside the boundaries of time."

My head was starting to hurt, but I nodded to indicate I was following him.

"Every Christian," Paul noted, "is immersed into Christ at the moment of salvation and joins with Him in His death.[166] This means that when Jesus gave up His spirit, we were *with* Him, in His body."

The thought was sobering. Execution was what I deserved because of my sins against God. Jesus gave His life in my place.

I could guess where Paul was going with this lesson: He was headed to Jerusalem not because he wanted to go but because the Holy Spirit was prompting his heart. And because Paul chose total obedience to the will of the One who had made such a great sacrifice on our behalf, Paul was determined to serve faithfully—even if that service led him to his demise.

"Because of my co-crucifixion with Christ," Paul continued, "I no longer allow this world—what I want, even what other believers want—to control me.[167] The world has been crucified to me, and I to the world."[168]

I tried to smile, hoping to bring some levity to our heavy conversation. "The world is not all bad, is it? The Lord made it, after all."

One corner of his mouth lifted. "There is much beauty in the world, yes. But I consider myself dead to this world and all this age has to offer because my citizenship is in heaven.[169] I am alive to God, but I am dead to this world. His plans for me must always outweigh all others."

That was his final answer, then. Paul would go to Jerusalem no matter what I or anyone else said. He cared little for our opinion; Paul lived solely to please Jesus.

I decided to change the topic. Last night the faces of two beautiful women swirled in my dreams. "Is it wrong for me to make plans of my own?" I asked. "Plans for a home and a family here on earth?"

Paul took a long glance at me and smiled, teasing lighting his eyes. "'Do not lay up for yourselves treasures on earth,'[170] he quoted Jesus' teachings. But then he reached over and patted my shoulder. "No, Timothy. That's not wrong. Marriage and family are the Lord's creations and blessings to be used for His glory. Just because God designed a certain plan for my life does not mean yours must look the same."

I nodded.

"Are you thinking of Bayla or Shayna?" he asked. "I've seen you read that letter at least a hundred times."

"I'm just thinking about the topic in general," I answered quickly. *Perhaps our previous topic is safer.* "Tell me more about what it means to be dead to this world, please. I'd like to understand that more clearly."

"It means," he replied, taking the bait, "that I don't have to worry about my things being stolen, and I don't need many things anyway. It means I am at ease with life and what happens to me. I don't care if they put me in jail. I am certainly not afraid of dying. I realize that my heavenly reward will far exceed even the best of what I can experience here, and I allow the joy of pleasing the Lord to drive my choices."

"I don't know, Paul. Some might say that's extreme."

"Jesus Himself told us to take up our cross every day,"[171] he replied. "When we die to this world—letting go of all of its things and ways—God gives incredible peace. Through faith in Christ, we overcome this world[172] and know the next one will be better."

I cocked my head sideways and said, "I thought we were supposed to love the world."

"As a Christian, I am supposed to love people living in the world, but not the world itself. This world is only temporary.[173] Why invest in something that is passing away? Second, the whole world lies under the sway of the wicked one.[174] Why would I allow myself to be lured by the Devil's playthings? Third, when I love the world, I allow culture to squeeze me into its mold.[175] Why should I let the world dominate me? Christ died to set me free from this evil age."[176]

His words resonated with me.

"When I remember my co-crucifixion with Christ, Timothy, I experience incredible bliss.[177] I no longer count my life on earth so dear.[178] Instead, I experience serenity, a peaceful sense that no matter what might happen in my future here on earth, I can trust that I'm in God's hands. No need to worry. No need to panic. Should my death happen soon, He will welcome me home."

Only days later Philip and his family walked us to the edge of town, closer to Paul's destiny in Jerusalem. Wary, yet determined to follow my friend as he followed Christ's leading, I stood well away from the hugs and handshakes offered us and quickly moved down the trail. Once a safe distance away, I turned and waved good-bye. I was surprised by Bayla's expression; she looked just as dejected at our parting as I felt when I first left Shayna in Ephesus.

Feeling a bit sorry for her, yet having made up my mind, I gave her a small smile and nodded once in farewell.

A sense of dread snaked around my heart as we walked up to Jerusalem. Silas looked just as tense as I felt. A flock of hunched over buzzards sat on a snag, watching us as we passed under their tree. Paul, many paces ahead of us, whistled a tune and seemed oblivious to the danger ahead.

"We've been calling him 'the man who won't stay dead' for years," I said to Silas, walking alongside him and gesturing in Paul's direction. "Should the worst come, I sure hope the Lord will return Paul to us."

"He may," Silas answered. "But then again, He may not."

Grow as a Disciple:

Paul explained to Timothy that the cross is not just for Jesus; it is also for Christians. What did he mean when he said that we are crucified with Christ? _____

_____

What three reasons does Paul give against falling in love with the world? _____

_____

In practical terms, how does a Christian "die" every day?

_____

_____

It has been said, "The Christian has to work hard to enter God's rest." Is this statement true or false? Explain. _____

_____

_____

Memory Verse:

Commit either Isaiah 26:3 or Galatians 6:14 to memory. Write here for practice. _____

_____

_____

Prepare to Disciple Others:

What encouragement might you give to a Christian who came to you, stressed by international news of persecution and his government's response to it? _____

_____

_____

Chapter 9

DISCOVERING LIBERTY

A.D. 60

After taking care of some personal business, Luke joined us in the Holy City of Jerusalem and was apprised quickly of Agabus's prophecy as well as Paul's determination to minister there anyway. Luke, Silas, and I hoped Paul would play it safe, but it seemed he was determined never to do that again. Sometimes I found myself feeling more like Paul's parent and bodyguard than the boy he'd taken under his tutelage in Lystra so long ago.

Only two weeks after our arrival, Luke caught my arm in a panic. His presence was unexpected because I'd thought he and the others were working across town while I sat teaching a small group of believers. "They arrested Paul," he whispered, trying not to disturb my class. "They've arrested *Paul!*"

We stared at each other for a moment, not surprised but sickened the inevitable had happened so quickly. I blew out a long breath, dismissed my group, and asked Luke to take me to our fearless leader. Somehow I knew things would never be the same for our small missionary band.

After a few days, the officials took Paul to Caesarea, where he would spend two *years* in prison. As a result of the incarceration, Paul saw the fulfillment of a prophecy from the earliest days of his ministry; in it the Lord foretold that he would bear the name of Christ before kings.[179] Sure enough, amidst great pomp, he was able to share with King Agrippa, Bernice, commanders, and prominent men of the city, as well as governors Felix and Festus.[180]

Silas, Luke, and I visited Paul regularly during this season, ministering to the other prisoners as we cared for Paul. We gave the inmates hope and encouragement through the Lord Jesus Christ, choosing to believe the Lord could use even Paul's confinement as an opportunity to spread the gospel message. He had, after all, orchestrated the salvation of a Roman jailer and his whole family less than a decade prior.

One day an interesting visitor arrived in Caesarea: the infamous John Mark. To my surprise, I liked him right away. He wasn't the bad guy I had once assumed. Instead, he was a pleasant man, with a round face and round eyes. He was polished and kind, and it didn't take me long to realize he was a scholar in his own right.

Over the course of a week, John Mark visited Paul several times at the prison, patching up old grievances and renewing their friendship. At the close of the Lord's Day, Paul announced that he wanted John Mark and Silas to go visit the churches up north. I was a little sorry to see Silas paired with another for such an assignment, for he'd been a tremendous encouragement to me over the years I'd been traveling and finding my footing as a missionary. There was no guarantee I'd see him again. Still, I agreed with Paul's choice: Silas was the ideal person to reintroduce John Mark to missionary life. John Mark was eager for a second chance, merrily accepting Paul's terms. He and Silas went on their way, while Luke and I stayed close to Paul.

Meanwhile, rumor had it Jewish radicals were conspiring to murder our friend. Things got particularly tense one day when Paul was ordered to stand before Governor Festus. Several Jews came down from Jerusalem, lodging false charges against him. To avoid their assassination attempt, Paul appealed to Caesar.[181]

A Roman centurion named Julius was assigned to take Paul to

Rome where he would have his chance to stand before the emperor.[182] Luke and I asked to go with Paul on the voyage, and Julius agreed to allow it. Unfortunately, although Julius treated us with kindness,[183] it proved unwise to sail so late in the season.[184] Our voyage was no pleasure cruise—not that we expected such under the circumstances.

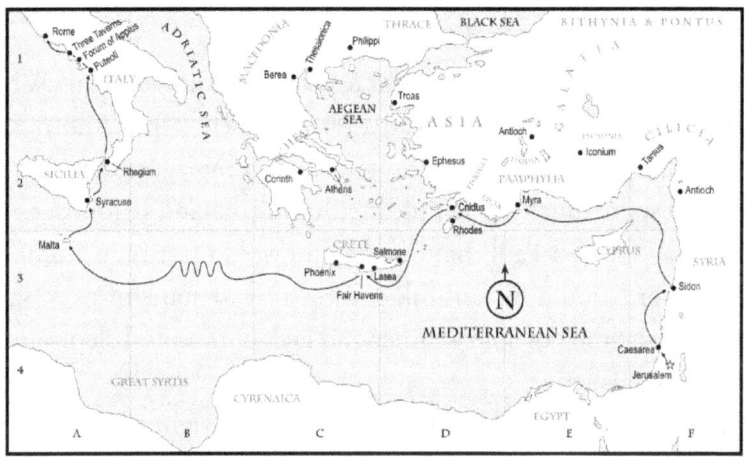

First we sailed on a fine little ship from Adramyttium, staying as close as possible to the shoreline since the winds were contrary. When we stopped safely in Lycia, Julius found us a bigger Alexandrian ship headed for Rome. This large, three-masted vessel carried grain from Egypt. While it looked safe and was certainly more spacious than our earlier conveyance, it soon proved us fools for leaving Myra.

On our first day out the conditions looked promising, a pleasant breeze blew in from the south. Not long after Myra slipped from view, however, a fierce storm arose. Cold, driving winds from the northeast, known as Euroclydon, pushed us way off course.[185] The extreme weather made the voyage perilous. At times the waves were as high as small mountains, terrorizing even the most seasoned sailors. When we dipped down in the trough below such a wave, all we could see were massive walls of water on every side. The wooden vessel creaked and groaned under the pressure as wave after wave crashed down, threatening to wipe the deck clean of even the sailors who'd lashed themselves to the masts. Those of us who could stayed below deck as ordered.

After several days of such pounding by the weather, the sailors became concerned and threw overboard all excess cargo, hoping to lighten our load and ease our way. But still, for many days the sun didn't shine and the storm didn't stop. Our sails tattered and our men exhausted, we were adrift, more or less lost at sea. All meal service stopped, and for two weeks we didn't eat a bite:[186] for most, starvation seemed preferable to facing further horrors.

By this time most of the men were afraid and despondent. While I certainly had my moments of fear, I remembered to put into practice the Royal Prayer Grandma had taught me so long ago. And, like Paul and Luke, I spent much of my time meditating on God's promises. After all, God had assured Paul that one day he would testify in Rome.[187] I knew the Lord would be faithful, getting at least some of us to safety. And so, despite the horrible weather and lack of rations, I slept soundly as the waves crashed.

On the fifteenth day we finally came within sight of an unknown island. All two-hundred-and-seventy-six of us had a bite to eat, and then the sailors threw some wheat overboard to lighten us further as they aimed the ship toward an inlet. That strip of land was one of the most beautiful sights on earth.

I stood at the side, enjoying the view and the relatively calm day, but I should have been holding on. When our ship ran aground on a reef,[188] I went flying into the sea. While I have little memory of what happened next, I was told I hit my head on something in the water when I fell. Whatever it was must have knocked me out cold, because I was soon sinking to the bottom under a trail of bubbles. Thankfully, a quick-thinking sailor pulled me out and dragged me to shore where Luke beat my back to expel the water and propped me against a tree so I could catch my breath.

Remarkably, everyone survived the sea voyage, some swimming to safety and others floating to the shore on top of planks and other debris.[189]

The island, we found, was called Malta.[190] The people there received us with kindness and made a large fire to comfort us. To show our gratitude, everyone from the shipwreck gathered wood and threw it on the roaring fire. The warmth of the blaze and the solid ground under our feet felt wonderful.

I had just sat down at the fire to enjoy a hastily prepared meal offered by the natives when Paul approached the blaze with a bundle of sticks in his arms. As he dropped them into the flames, a snake seemed to leap from the pile, sinking its tiny fangs into his hand. Several people gasped at the sight, probably thinking the event was an omen that Paul was a murderer whom fate had chosen to kill with or without the sea's help. But Paul just shook the viper off and, amazingly, suffered no harm. The natives hailed him as a god; Paul used their misunderstanding as a chance to tell them about the true God and His Son.[191]

In the days that followed, God used Paul the prisoner to preach the gospel and to bring miraculous healing to others in Malta. Three months later, Julius had secured our transportation to Rome; it was a big grain ship that would take us to Syracuse, Rhegium, and finally to Puteoli. By the time we set sail, Malta's locals happily supplied all the provisions needed.[192]

Upon our arrival in Puteoli, Julius announced we would walk the final distance to Rome. All along our journey, we met Christians who had caught word of the famed apostle's coming. Some invited us to stay with them, and remarkably, even Paul was allowed to do so. At Three Inns, which is simply a rest stop made up of three stores on the Appian Way, the believers came out from Rome and welcomed Paul. They knew him by reputation and by his letter to the church at Rome, and they wanted to encourage him in his chains. Their efforts and love blessed him deeply.[193]

As Luke and I walked alongside our friend during that stretch, I noticed how much Paul had aged. He still loved to be with people all day long—was energized by their presence, in fact—but he was slower in movement and his face had taken on new lines. The travel, I realized, was hard on him.

It was growing increasingly wearing on me too, I admitted, though my struggles were not tied to my age as much as they were to my heart. I'd been writing to Shayna for many long months, and we were promised to one another. "There's no one for me but you," she'd written in her last letter. "I'll follow you wherever the Lord leads." Still, I knew I was in no position to marry. As long as Paul was imprisoned, I would remain close to serve him. Thankfully, Shayna supported that.

Upon our arrival in Rome, the capital city set on hillsides and boasting a million citizens, the soldiers confined Paul to house arrest while he awaited trial.[194] Though he wasn't allowed to leave his dwelling and was chained to a guard much of the time, the arrangement itself was far preferable to its alternate: sitting in a dark dungeon alone. After such a miserable winter, Paul needed to rest and recover, but his busy schedule never slowed. In those weeks, it seemed half of Rome's citizens came out to see Paul the great apostle, and Paul made time for everyone.[195]

One day an old friend named Epaphras came along with the horde of visitors. Paul invited him to stay with us that night so we'd have uninterrupted time together once night fell.

We'd first met Epaphras years earlier in Ephesus while teaching at the School of Tyrannus. In the years since, Epaphras had carried the gospel into the Lycus Valley. Then, following Paul's church-starting methods, he planted a church in Colossae.[196] All went well, he reported, until religious imposters infiltrated the congregation there.

"I need your counsel," Epaphras said as we waited for Luke to arrive with food. He'd headed out to gather a feast fit for honored company. "I've traveled all the way to Rome to seek your advice."[197]

Paul leaned forward, his black, bushy eyebrows lowered. Clearly he was angry about what Epaphras had shared about religious imposters hurting the church in Colossae. He had such passion for the churches—even those he'd never visited.[198] "And just who are these false teachers plaguing your flock?" he asked. "Is this more work by Nicolas DoM, that Dumb, obnoxious Man?"

Epaphras seemed surprised by the words, but I didn't flinch at Paul's vocal contempt for Nicolas. I'd heard his frustrations spill out before.[199]

He was very protective of the churches, and Nicolas had proven himself a wolf set on terrorizing them with misinformation.

"No, it's not Nicolas this time," Epaphras said. "He's formed a new group—the Nicolaitans they call themselves. I've heard they are off on a different tangent now."

"Then who are these false teachers in Colossae?" Paul pressed.

"Some of Nicolas's *old* group, the Defenders of Moses," our visitor clarified. "They told my church in Colossae that you cannot sever the tree from the trunk. Christianity grew out of Judaism, they insist, and therefore it is illogical to think Christians can divorce themselves from their Jewish heritage. Observances of certain holy days, dietary laws, and circumcision are *essential* to the Christian faith, they say."

Lucius, Paul's night guard, yawned at this point. Unlike Maximus the morning guard, who constantly weighed our words as if gathering information to use against us, Lucius seemed to think Paul—and his views—harmless. Though he'd heard Paul share the gospel hundreds of times, he didn't seem to think it applied to him. I liked the young soldier and it made me sad that he was so closed to our message, but his disinterest was a blessing in moments like this.

"Paul, my people are confused," Epaphras admitted.

"I'm really concerned, Paul," I broke in. "We might lose another church to the Judaizers.[200] The Defenders of Moses are at it again, overemphasizing the importance of the law."

"But the law of Moses isn't totally bad," Paul offered, his tone back to its earlier calm. "The law is good when used in the right way. We mustn't think of the law itself as our problem."

Epaphras contemplated on this for a moment and sighed. "Well, I'll tell you," he said. "I'm so weary of arguing against this Defenders of Moses bunch that I sometimes wonder whether I'm in the wrong after all. Maybe they know something I don't. Tell me, Paul. Please, refresh my memory. What *is* the proper use of the law?"

The apostle thought for a moment, watching Epaphras carefully. Clearly he was saddened by the man's admission that the agitators were making him question his own views. "Before I explain how the law should function," he began, "let me share with you two ways people misuse the law. Some try to use the law as a means of justification, and others try to use the law as a means of sanctification. Both are wrong."

"Before you go on," Epaphras said, "will you define those terms in plain language? Some of my people struggle to understand words like *justification* and *sanctification*."

Paul nodded. "Justification refers to legal righteousness. A person is justified when God declares him not guilty because of his faith in the death, burial, and resurrection of Jesus Christ.

"Sanctification refers to practical righteousness. A sanctified Christian is one who lives a holy, circumspect life and demonstrates power over temptation." He smiled at our guest. "Does that help?"

Epaphras nodded.

"First," Paul continued, "some people believe they must keep the law in order to be saved or declared righteous in the eyes of the Lord. They think they must obey the precepts of God to prove they are worthy of heaven."

"But you cannot show me one person who has ever achieved righteousness by obedience to the law,"[201] I offered, remembering what I'd been taught. "No one, except Jesus, has ever kept all the law. Only God is good."

"Well said, Timothy," Paul affirmed. "Even a man who counts himself very good by his own standards is imperfect. Because if a person could manage to keep all the laws, but broke only one, that would make him a lawbreaker. In order to be justified by the law, a person has to keep the whole law."[202]

"And Jesus said there will not be any lawbreakers in heaven,"[203] I supplied.

"I understand that we have no hope apart from grace," Epaphras said. "But why did the Lord give us 613 laws through Moses if He meant to retire them after Christ appeared? I'm asked that question all the time, and to be honest, I'm not certain how to respond."

"The 613 laws of Moses are detailed, exhaustive, and overwhelming,"

Paul answered, reaching for his cup. "They remain as proof that we need a Savior. We Jews have never been justified by the law. Our father Abraham believed God; then God declared him righteous because of his faith.[204] God justified Abraham apart from the law. The law did not even exist until 430 years later.[205] That's important."

"If righteousness comes through the law, then Christ died in vain,"[206] I added.

"That's right," Paul affirmed. "And besides that, the Council of Jerusalem convened a few years ago to settle this very issue. The apostles and elders there talked about the Gentile's relationship to the law. The council agreed Gentiles are not required to obey all the laws of Moses in order to become Christians. They affirmed salvation by grace through faith and then distributed a written report to the churches."[207]

"I've read it," our guest said. "The troublemakers know all about it too."

"Yet those legalists in Colossae continue to stir up trouble?" I asked, though I knew the answer.

Epaphras nodded. Our enemies were determined. "I'd hoped that by learning more about this topic I might be in a better position to defend the flock," he said. "Paul, you mentioned that people misuse the law in two ways. What is the second?"

"Sometimes people use the law in a vain attempt to achieve justification, as we just discussed. Other times, people use the law to try to achieve sanctification. These misguided souls think they become better Christians if they obey a bunch of restrictions. Often they come up with ridiculous man-made rules. They regulate marriage, holy days, food, and drink. Sometimes they bring back Jewish laws such as circumcision. One way or another, they come up with a list of do's and don'ts.

"The point is that moral checklists do not make anyone a better person. Severe treatment of the body is not the way to godliness. Rules and regulations do not make us more like Jesus. I don't care how pious, devoted, or disciplined a person may be; those forms of religion will not conquer evil desires,"[208] he said.

"Second, legalists trying to achieve sanctification presume to add to Christ. They imply that to be a good Christian one needs Jesus plus something else, which is offensive and wrong. Believers are complete in Christ.[209] Jesus is all anyone needs.

"And third, the way to live a good Christian life is not with more rules, but by trusting in Jesus. The righteousness of God is revealed from faith to faith.[210] Both justification and sanctification are the result of faith in Christ.[211] We do not begin the Christian life by faith and then continue the Christian life with the works of the law. Christianity involves faith from start to finish.[212] As the prophet Habakkuk said, 'The just shall live by his faith.'"[213]

I opened my mouth to respond, but the wooden door at the front of the house swung open and in marched Luke, carrying a basket of food. "I've got supper," he announced, oblivious to the depth of our conversation.

Paul gave thanks for the meal. Then, when Luke opened the basket, I smelled the aroma of fresh baked bread. He soon pulled forth goat cheese, cucumbers, tomatoes, honey, and raisins. For several minutes we and the guard ate and talked of lighter subjects until I steered our conversation back to the purpose of our guest's visit. I asked Paul to explain the proper use of the law.

Our friend wiped his plate clean with the flatbread, sopping up every last drop of honey. "The purpose of the law is very simple," he said. "Two stories, one about a schoolboy and another about a widow, will help you see how we should relate to it."

Luke, Epaphras, and I kept eating and listened as Paul continued. Lucius studied the cracks in the walls.

"Once upon a time, a wealthy man wanted his son educated, so he enlisted his most-trusted slave and instructed him to escort his son to the school where the Rabbi taught. This went on daily for some time, and the slave kept the little boy under strict control as he walked him to and from school every day. But as time passed, the son grew old enough that he no longer need the slave to walk him to school. He matured to the point where he saw the value of an education, loved the

Rabbi, and would go straight to school alone, thus no longer needing the assistance of his father's slave.

"In this story, the wealthy man represents our heavenly Father; the slave represents the law; the schoolboy represents us; and the Rabbi symbolizes Jesus.[214] Based on the story, Timothy, what is the purpose of the law?"

"The function of the law is to get us to Jesus."

"Very good. You see, the law defines sin,[215] reveals sin,[216] and points individuals to the Savior. And as the story shows, when a person connects with Christ, he no longer needs the law.[217] The law is not for Christians but for sinners.[218] It helps wicked people realize they need a Savior."

"Yes, that illustration is very good!" Epaphras enthused. "I can use that. But you also mentioned a story about a widow. What's that about?"

"The law is in effect over a person until nullified by death." Paul rubbed his eyes, a motion that had long been a habit. "For example, a woman is bound to her husband while he lives. She can't marry anyone else because the law binds her to him. But if her husband dies, she is free from the law that held her, and she can legally remarry.[219]

"In the same way, when we accept Christ's gift of salvation and die in Him, we are set free from the law. And if we die with Christ to this world, why would we want to go back to rudimentary teachings such as, 'Do this,' 'Don't do that,' 'Don't touch that,' and 'Don't eat that'?[220] If Christ has set you free, stand firm, and don't go back to the yoke of slavery."[221]

"So," Epaphras asked, "because my people and I are free from the law, we no longer need try to please God with our works of righteousness?"

"Exactly," Paul enthused. "We do the right thing to show gratitude and to express our love for Him, not to earn His love. You may consider our old way of life—that way of trying to earn God's approval through our own righteousness, offering sacrifices, and giving alms—nothing but rubbish."[222]

Paul continued to talk, but my mind began to wander. It had been a long few weeks, and my attitude had bordered on sour for days. Our conversation troubled me. *If we aren't under the law,* I asked myself, *why do we just sit back and allow the abuses like those Epaphras faces? Why tolerate the injustice Paul deals with daily when forced to sit in this house—especially when he must be chained to that mean-spirited Maximus?* When I considered how to reverse the immediate situation and carried the thought to its extreme, a diabolical plan began to emerge.

The time would come when I'd see with clarity that my idea came from the Devil. But in that moment, as I thought about how weary I was of my friend's imprisonment and how anxious I was to finally marry Shayna, I told myself that since I was free from the law, I had the right to fight for justice.

Grow as a Disciple:

Paul explained to Timothy that Christians have "died" and are now "free" from the law. What, then, is the purpose of the law? _____

_____

_____

List some man-made rules people use to justify themselves or to earn God's favor. _____

_____

_____

Describe the attitudes and actions of a legalistic person. Then list reasons why legalism is dangerous.

Memory Verse:

Commit to memory either Galatians 2:21 or Galatians 5:1. Write here for practice. _____

_____

_____

Prepare to Disciple Others:

Suppose a man came to you who had just come out of a cult and professed faith in Christ as Savior. He is upset because some church members enjoy worldly forms of entertainment he considers questionable. How would you respond? _____

_____

_____

_____

Chapter 10

DISCOVERING
VICTORY

A.D. 61

My dislike for Paul's guard Maximus couldn't be traced to any one thing. True, he was a suspicious, grumpy character—difficult to get along with even on his best day. But he also was mean and behaved like a buffoon. After only a few weeks of his presence in the tiny house where Paul lived, I came to cringe at the sight of the Roman's squinty eyes, bulbous red nose, and missing front teeth. Unlike the other guards who passed their service hours with either quiet respect or genuine disinterest in the happenings around them, Maximus harassed Paul, stirred up trouble, and ridiculed the faith. Many times I wondered how a gentle, loving man like my mentor could be imprisoned when thugs like Maximus roamed freely.

Paul was kind to his guards, and over the months of his house arrest, many had become followers of Christ as their work forced them to spend days within earshot of him delivering sermons, teaching lessons, reading letters intended for the churches, and praying even for his captors. Even so, Maximus loudly taunted and harassed Paul to the point that Paul could no longer write or teach when under Maximus's watchful eye.

Paul handled the situation well and treated Maximus with respect, shifting his visits and writing time to the late afternoons when a different guard stood watch. Most afternoons, we tried to keep the house quiet because Paul and Luke were writing extensively during that time. Paul—sometimes requesting my help—penned letters to the Colossians, to a man named Philemon, to the Ephesians, and to the Philippians. Luke wrote a two-part historical summary to his friend Theophilus. The first he called "The Gospel According to Luke;" the second was "The Acts of the Apostles." When I wasn't working with Paul on his letters, I was often the errand runner, keeping an eye on Maximus as I came and went. So great was his hostility that I half expected him to burn the house down over our heads. I refused to let such a thing happen.

The morning after Epaphras's visit, I was still angry. I'd slept little, frustrated by news of what was happening in his church and still toying with the idea of using my freedom from the law to its fullest advantage. Deep down I knew what I contemplated wasn't right. It wasn't in line with my beliefs as one who sought to follow Christ's example, but I tasted bile when Maximus arrived for his shift. Not only did he reek of beer, but the first thing he did—with no warning at all—was spit on one of Paul's precious scrolls.

Rage filled me as Maximus took his position beside Paul, closing one end of the apostle's constant iron bracelet around his own wrist. Realizing he was distracted with securing the lock, I saw my opportunity. Almost without conscious thought, I felt my fingertips slide around the smooth ivory handle of my dagger. Slowly, quietly, I pulled the knife from the scabbard at my side. I was behind our enemy, and he wasn't paying a bit of attention to me.

My blood thumping in my ears, I took a step toward him. Then another.

And another.

I raised my weapon.

"Timothy!" Paul suddenly shouted, his voice bright and loud.

My heart in my throat, I hid the knife behind me in one quick motion, thankful Maximus had not turned around fast enough to see. Startled and burning with shame over the rebuke I saw in Paul's eyes, I abandoned my plan and went to the market to purchase the fruit he requested.

For the remainder of the week, I vainly hoped Paul would remain so busy with people that he wouldn't have time to scold me. It seemed, for a while, that my hopes might come true. When Paul wasn't writing letters, he was hosting the parade of Christians that streamed through the house. Many of the visitors only came occasionally. But there were others, besides myself and Luke, who were regulars: Tychicus, Aristarchus, Justus, Demas, Onesimus, Epaenetus, Mary, Urbanus, Apelles, Persis, Hermas, Olympas, Epaphroditus, and many more.[223] But I knew that sooner or later, I would have to face the apostle's fury. I was a trusted missionary, and I had nearly undermined everything we as Christians were meant to accomplish.

The more I thought about it, the more I realized how stupidly I had behaved. I could've sent a man into eternity without the Lord. I could've been killed. I could've gotten Paul killed. The witness of the church, and worse, the Lord's name, could've been horribly tarnished. How disappointed Shayna would be to know what I had attempted. Would I throw away my life, losing any chance of becoming her long-awaited bridegroom? Had I learned nothing in all my years with Paul?

My overdue lecture came one warm summer afternoon when Paul and I were practically alone. Paul's afternoon guard, Antony, was sound asleep at his side. Most likely he would stay that way until mealtime.

I knew the apostle was about to talk about the incident of days before because his eyes were filled not with the usual affection for me but with raw disappointment. I launched into my defense before he could get started. "Paul, before you say anything about what happened, know that I am sorry. I shouldn't have been so impulsive, but I remember you said we are free from the law, so I thought perhaps it was time to...."

Paul raised his free hand and stopped me mid-sentence. "No, Timothy, my son. Do not make excuses. You are free from the law, but you know from our Lord's example that you must never use your

135

freedom as an excuse to indulge your flesh.[224] What happened last week was unacceptable."

His words brought to mind Jesus, quiet in the face of accusation, turning His cheek rather than retaliating, offering forgiveness to the very people who'd so callously nailed Him to a tree. "You are right, Paul," I nodded. "Truly, I am so sorry. I'll never do anything like that again."

Paul asked me to push his quill and ink closer. When I did, he began to draw on a piece of parchment as I held it steady for him— an arrangement familiar to both of us. Near the top of the page he wrote *Jesus Christ* and penned the word *Christian* at the bottom; the action reminded me of our connected circle lessons from years ago. But this sketch looked a little different. This time there were two lines descending from Christ's name, one on either side, and two ascending from the circle belonging to the Christ-follower, one on either side. Each side's lines crossed each other, creating two Xs on the scroll. In the middle of the X on the left, Paul drew a cross and labeled it *Death*. In the middle of the X on the right, he drew a crown and labeled it *Life*. In years to come that parchment would become one of my most treasured possessions.

In a soft voice, so as not to disturb the guard, Paul pointed to the crown and said, "We identify with Jesus Christ in both His life and death." He gestured to the cross at that last word.

"I remember," I said, trying not to hang my head in shame.

"Good." Paul shifted his weight and continued. "Timothy, in the years I've known you, I've seen you grow into a fine man of God. But the other day I saw you make a poor choice. You forgot that the old you, that angry fellow who liked a good fight, is gone. Though you belong to Christ, you were ready to resurrect your sin nature."

I nodded. He was right. For an awful moment I'd allowed the thought of revenge to override better sense and to pull me right back into old ways. I'd forgotten that sin is sin. And because I am crucified in Christ, I have no business choosing vengeance—whether I feel free to do so or not.

"Think of Timothy before he met Christ as a man whose life is over," Paul said. "Then tell me. Can you tempt a dead person to do wrong?"

I wrinkled my face. "No, of course not. A dead man can't be tempted."

"Truth," he smiled with a bit of the twinkle I'd grown to miss playing around his eyes. "By faith we understand that at the moment of our conversion, God placed us into Christ. Our old sinful nature, then, is crucified because of our union with the Lord. Though we will at times be tempted to go back to it, we are wise to remember that at the cross our sinful nature was dealt a deadly blow. Sin can no longer dominate us."[225]

"But sometimes the old Timothy *does* raise his ugly head, Paul," I admitted. "Sometimes he is tempted, though dead as you say."

He thought about that for a moment. "Perhaps it would be best to say the old nature has been mortally wounded. Just as crucifixion is an event and a process, there may be an initial mortification of the flesh, but death to self must happen every day.[226] As you know, victims of crucifixion may remain alive for several days on the cross. When Jesus hung on one, in fact, the enemy tempted Him to come down off the cross prematurely,[227] but Jesus chose to stay. We have to do the same. Because our old nature will struggle to reassert itself, we have to continually remind ourselves of our crucifixion with Christ. Every day, by faith, we must embrace the cross and consider ourselves dead to sin.[228] Thus, we no longer have to obey our old sinful nature."

"We find victory," I said, realizing more clearly than ever that daily victory would require an ongoing choice to remember my union with Christ on the cross.

"Absolutely," he affirmed. "But I don't mean to suggest crucifixion of the flesh is effortless. If I've made this sound trouble free, then it's my turn to apologize. It's not easy. In fact, putting your flesh to death is war. The Spirit and flesh fight against each other daily[229]—the flesh longing to be pampered and the Spirit desiring to keep in step with God's plans."[230]

"I want to live in victory, Paul," I told him, and I meant it.

Our conversation immediately lifted the tension in the little house where Paul stayed, and I expected things to return to their normal routine. I was surprised when the next day Paul looked up from his writings, set down his quill, and said, "My letter to the Philippians is almost complete. Will you deliver it for me?"[231]

I nodded that I would, not realizing Paul had another reason for sending me to Philippi. Though Epaphroditus, Tychicus, or even the runaway slave Onesimus could have just as easily delivered the letter en route to Macedonia, [232] Paul wanted me to go because he suspected it might give me a chance to improve a particular relationship, perhaps even giving me a renewed opportunity to share Jesus. Maximus, the surly guard, had received new orders and would travel a path similar to mine for part of his journey. Clearly his superiors thought it was time for him to move on to more active duty.

As soon as I heard the news, I felt ill and knew I needed to find a quiet, private place to pray. *"Dear God,"* I began, *"You have told me to regard myself dead to sin but alive to You in Christ Jesus.[233] So right now, by faith, I am agreeing with You. God, I put to death my feelings of hatred toward Maximus.[234] I choose to die to self so Jesus can live through me.[235] Because of my co-crucifixion with Christ, I consider my old nature dead, and I understand I don't have to obey its sinful lusts. With Your help, Lord, I now choose to forgive Maximus. Please, help me to extend him Your grace and kindness. In Jesus' name, amen."*

Later in the week, I got an opportunity to put my faith into action when Maximus showed up for duty. In spite of the near end of his time as a guard in Paul's tiny dwelling, he arrived hungover and just as grumpy as usual. His bloodshot eyes shot daggers of disgust at us from the moment he entered the room.

After Maximus sat down and got locked into place, I spoke. "May I get you a cup of water, Maximus?"

The hairy soldier stared at me, opened his mouth to say something unpleasant, but then abruptly paused—apparently rendered speechless. These were my first kind words to him in a long time. After a moment, he grunted in assent. Secretly pleased, I walked over to the cistern and ladled him a cup of water. When I handed it to him, he mumbled something that could have been thanks and drank deeply as if he hadn't had water in days.

For the first time ever, I felt compassion for the man and asked to refill his cup when he finished. When he accepted that second drink with only a trace of his usual surliness, a marvelous sense of joy washed over my soul. I knew that by dying to my personal dislikes in order to serve Maximus, I had won a huge spiritual victory.

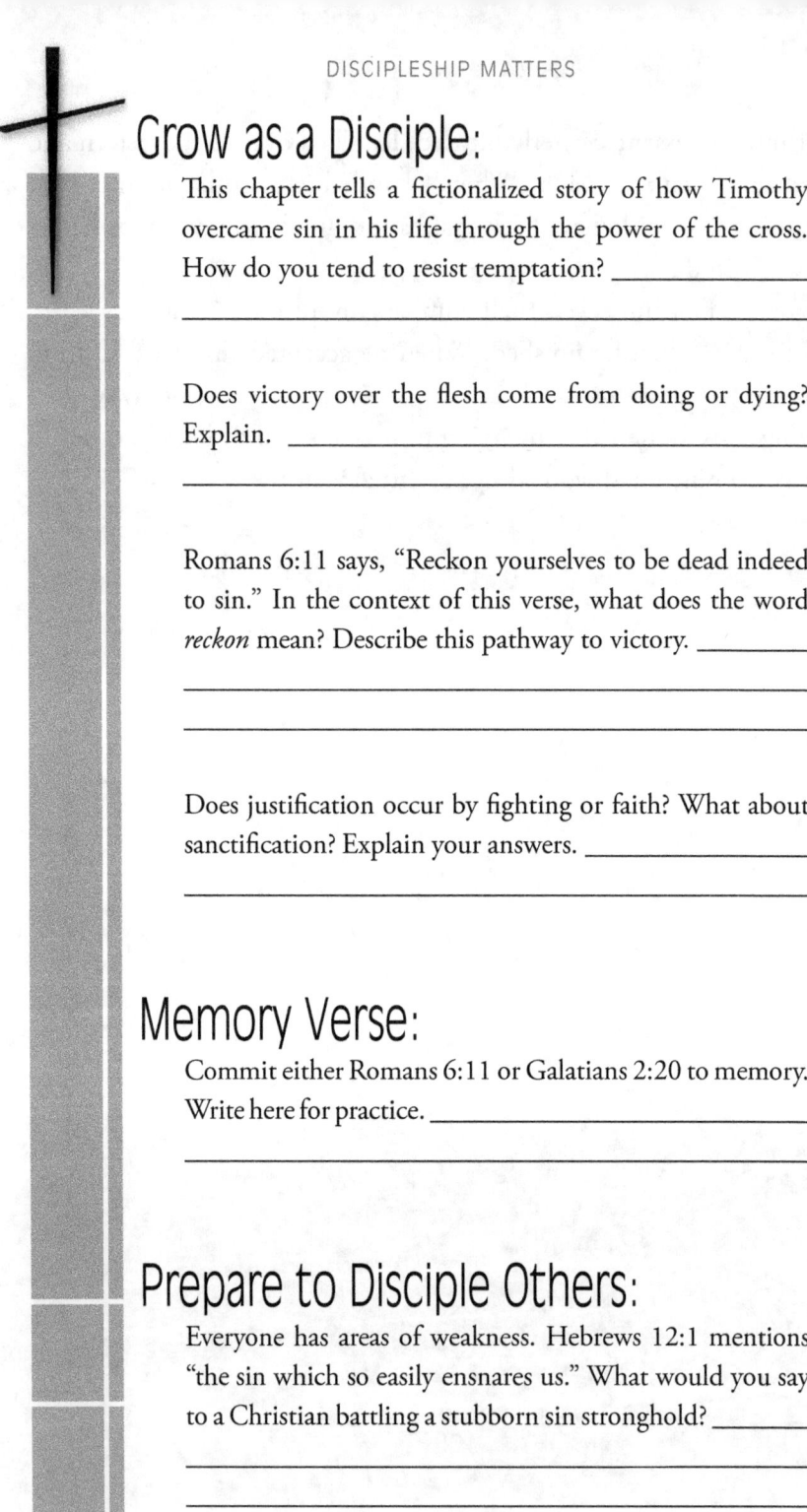

Grow as a Disciple:

This chapter tells a fictionalized story of how Timothy overcame sin in his life through the power of the cross. How do you tend to resist temptation? _____

_____

Does victory over the flesh come from doing or dying? Explain. _____

_____

Romans 6:11 says, "Reckon yourselves to be dead indeed to sin." In the context of this verse, what does the word *reckon* mean? Describe this pathway to victory. _____

_____

_____

Does justification occur by fighting or faith? What about sanctification? Explain your answers. _____

_____

Memory Verse:

Commit either Romans 6:11 or Galatians 2:20 to memory. Write here for practice. _____

_____

Prepare to Disciple Others:

Everyone has areas of weakness. Hebrews 12:1 mentions "the sin which so easily ensnares us." What would you say to a Christian battling a stubborn sin stronghold? _____

_____

_____

_____

Chapter 11

DISCOVERING CHRIST'S INHERITANCE

A.D. 62

After two years of house arrest in Rome, Paul was released and his case dismissed. Those who'd accused him in Caesarea had not bothered to carry their arguments as far as the capitol.

When first he stepped out into the sunshine as a free man, my breath caught at the sight of him. He was permanently bent over and stoop-shouldered. His skin had grown sallow and creased from too much time spent sitting indoors. Five years of incarceration—two in Caesarea, two in Rome, plus the voyage between them—had left their marks on Paul's body.

Yet despite his poor posture and declining health, a passion still burned within Paul. He longed to see more churches started and others strengthened. Almost as soon as we left Rome, we began another missionary adventure. In those precious months on the road again, I felt as if we'd returned to old times—though I still missed Silas, and Luke did not accompany us.

Things did not stay pleasant for long. Unfortunately, during a visit to Ephesus, at which Shayna and I began to make formal wedding plans, we heard reports that an old thorn was still causing trouble for the churches. Almost ten years earlier Paul predicted that savage wolves would creep into the flock and do great damage.[236] And sure enough, corrupt men like Nicolas DoM had set up camp—even in large cities like Ephesus, misleading many with their twisted teachings. Though the Ephesian church had once enjoyed an unusual anointing upon their ministry, their fire and power had largely disappeared. The once-great church had stopped evangelizing their city in order to focus their energies inward. In ignoring the souls of lost people, they showed they had left their first love.[237]

Not long after we arrived in Ephesus, we set to repairing the damage. Paul and I loved, taught, and encouraged the believers. Soon most of them began to remember the importance of staying on mission, and we enjoyed speedy progress within the community and were gaining momentum.

One day while things were going well, I took Shayna on a picnic. Along for the adventure was Ruthie, the little girl who lived next door to Shayna whom we'd taken along as our chaperone. Shayna and I talked for hours, catching up on our years apart and planning for our future. I could have sat in the sunshine with my beloved until the sun went down, but the white kitten Ruthie had brought along got spooked and clawed its way up a sycamore tree. While Shayna laughed and Ruthie danced in anticipation of my success, I climbed up and rescued it.

Just as I made it back to the ground, Ezra, a young man from the church, ran toward us shouting my name. Breathless, he explained that I needed to follow him quickly. Paul wanted me.

It turned out that Paul needed my help breaking up a meeting held by our old enemy Nicolas DoM. As Shayna, Ruthie, and I hurried to keep up with the messenger, Ezra explained that his friend—once quite active in the church—had chosen to follow Nicolas's teachings. I learned that in the years since I'd seen him, Nicolas had undergone another "conversion," this time back to paganism. Now he and his new group, the Nicolaitans, were actively promoting idolatry and immorality wherever they went. An informant had let Paul know that professing Christians would be in attendance at the meeting that was just about to start.[238] Nicolas had lured them there on the pretense that he was leading a Scripture study.

"He would pull a stunt like this in the week leading up to Passover," Paul said once we reached Shayna's home where Paul and I stayed on the rooftop. "As you and I prepare the church to celebrate the death and resurrection of our Lord, Nicolas is turning people against the truth."

I agreed it was a terrible thing, said good-bye to Shayna and Ruthie, and followed Paul as he painfully made his way to the reported place of meeting. Though he was much slower than he once was, I always allowed him to lead.

We found Nicolas's small gathering and surprised him just as he was assuring a woman in attendance that her feelings for a man other than her husband might indicate that it was time to pursue a new partner. His words confirmed what we'd been told. Where once Nicolas had concerned himself with rule following, he was now just as likely to encourage people to seek truth through their feelings. We'd caught him in the act.

The church members we recognized seemed uneasy and confused by our entrance. Several looked as if they wanted to move for the door, but Nicolas motioned for them to stay seated. "You've heard me say," he addressed the group in his oily tone, "that Paul's preaching is too hard. It does not allow for the freedoms our God-given spirits rightly crave."

"Freedom is found in Christ," Paul stated calmly, his words depriving Nicolas's of their intended effect. The audience looked to Paul with awe and respect. Whereas Nicolas DoM was new in town, the Apostle Paul's reputation preceded him. If the great evangelist and writer had taken the time to interrupt their covert gathering, most of them likely realized, his message must be worthwhile.

For the next half hour, standing shoulder to shoulder, Paul and I confronted Nicolas with a quick retort against every point he made. I felt as if we were two foxes who'd cornered a striking snake.

"Feelings are important. We are wise to listen to them," Nicolas said.

"The prophet Jeremiah stated, 'The heart is deceitful above all things, and desperately wicked.'[239] Feelings are deceptive," Paul answered.

"Your teachings are too difficult. God wants people to have fun," Nicolas said as if he'd stated a fact.

"God wants us to be holy as He is holy,"[240] I insisted.

"You say you have freedom," Nicolas said, "yet you never allow for it. Avoid gluttony. Avoid accumulation. Avoid, avoid, that's all you unenlightened Christians do."

"In Christ we are free to obey God, free to serve others, free to enjoy life to its fullest, but we will not use our freedom to return to the bondage of sin," I said, thinking how ironic his point seemed considering his own legalistic past. *Ridiculous that he still uses the name DoM*, I mused, *now that he no longer cares about the laws of Moses.*

"If we sin, God will forgive us," Nicolas said.

"Yes," Paul replied. "That's true. But we must never presume on the grace of God."[241]

By this time Nicolas looked thoroughly annoyed and most of the crowd had lost interest in what he had to say. He cleared his throat and narrowed his eyes. The expression on his face suggested he thought he was about to deliver a fatal blow to our arguments. "Jesus said that in heaven there is no such thing as marriage. So why should anyone be bound to such outdated agreements now?"

I thought about my own upcoming marriage and realized the danger such thinking posed to families such as the one I planned to lead. "'Marriage *is* honorable among all, and the bed undefiled; but fornicators and adulterers God will judge.'[242] As Scripture states, in marriage a husband and wife are no longer two but one flesh. They are joined together by God. How could this design that began in the garden be flawed? The Lord always spoke of marriage with favor."[243]

A woman near the back of the room suddenly stood. Face white, she pointed a finger at Nicolas and said, "You never told me any of this!"

Things went downhill quickly for Nicolas from that point on. Not long after the meeting, Paul and I watched him leave town. When he threw a threatening gesture at us right before he disappeared from view, I grimaced and shook my head. Rumor had it he and his Nicolaitan band planned to head to Pergamos.[244] I prayed the church there would stand strong against his lies and schemes.

For a while Paul and I served together in Ephesus, me dividing my time between working for the church and accomplishing my goal of saving income to take care of Shayna. Serving as Paul's assistant pastor was exciting and rewarding, and Paul and I made a good team. But I often thought about how much more we'd accomplish once Shayna was at my side as constantly as her mother was at Aquila's. The three of us, I believed, would become an unstoppable force for God's kingdom.

I was totally unprepared for Paul's announcement that he would be moving on to Macedonia without me. "I want you to stay here in Ephesus and lead this church,"[245] he said at my protest, and I realized then that he already had his traveling pack at his feet. "The time has come for you to serve on your own."

I felt hot tears flood my eyes as a blur of emotions and objections swirled within me. Did Paul not realize how much he needed me? Had he not noticed that he was getting older and was not as strong as before? Did he have any idea how much this parting reminded me of the day my father unexpectedly walked away forever?

"I am not sure I'm qualified," I managed to say, my throat tight. "God made me an evangelist, Paul. I function best in an itinerant role."

He smiled, his face creased with kindness and love. "Timothy, do you remember the first time I sent you to Thessalonica by yourself?"

I nodded, wiping tears with the back of my hand.

He cupped my shoulder with his gnarled fingers and looked up to meet my eyes. "You served the Lord with excellence then, and since that time you have served on other missions with and without me.[246] You can do this, and you know you never face challenges alone. The Lord is in you, and you are in Him."[247]

In spite of myself, I felt my posture change from that of a frightened young boy to that of an obedient solider. I was no longer in training.

As Paul said, I was well qualified to pastor. I sniffed and agreed to do as he asked.

Paul expressed his pleasure by giving me a rare hug, and then his voice grew serious. "You have some big challenges here in Ephesus," he said, "so you must pray for God's help."

"I do pray, and I will."

"Of course," he smiled. "But from now on, when you pray, I urge you to pray from a new position."

"Should I kneel?" I asked.

"No, no. I'm not talking about bowing or lifting hands, though you certainly may. I did not say pray *in* a new position, but *from* a new position."

We sat down together and he continued. "As you bring your petitions before the Father, I want you to be mindful of your position in Christ. When you pray, remember you are in Christ, seated at the Father's right hand."

"I remember that lesson."

"Good. Now, don't be like some people who pray as though God were far away. You do not pray to a distant deity. In Christ, you are brought near by His blood.[248] Although you once were an alien and stranger to the Father, now you are a member of God's household. You know this, but you must always pray with it in mind."

"You are telling me this because you know that if I am mindful of my position in Christ, I will pray with greater assurance," I said.

Paul rubbed his bad eye and nodded, clearly pleased. He squinted at me. "Yes. Because the Father has adopted you into His royal family,[249] you can always cry out, 'Abba, Father,' anytime you have a need.[250] You once were a slave; but now you're a son.[251]

"As a child of the King, you have direct access to the Heavenly Father, and you can approach Him with confidence, even boldness.[252] As our Lord said, 'Your Father who is in heaven [will] give good things to those who ask Him!'[253] Because you are *in* Christ, you occupy a privileged position. When you are aware of your royal status, your faith increases and the quality of your prayers improve."

I'd heard him share much of this advice before during our years together, but I didn't mind the reminder. "I'll be sure to do that," I said.

Moments later we shook hands, preparing to go our separate ways, when he decided to add to his parting words. "One more thing, Timothy: always remember you are a coheir with Christ.[254] You, as a believer in Him, have an inheritance that far exceeds all the treasures of the world. Live with that in mind."

It was my turn to smile. While Christ didn't have much money during His lifetime on earth,[255] He did in fact own everything. Everything the Father has He has given to the Son.[256] And since I am in Christ, all those things are mine as well.[257] "In Christ, I have obtained a fantastic inheritance,"[258] I assured him. "Being in Christ means I have everything I need. I—and you—are blessed with every spiritual blessing in the heavenly places."[259]

"Indeed," Paul affirmed, obviously pleased that I was so carefully parroting wisdom gleaned from his work and our time together, "you are a wealthy man. And you can be sure God will supply every need of yours according to His riches in glory."[260]

He turned to go. "If you ever have a question," he said, "just remember: in Christ are all the treasures of wisdom and knowledge.[261] The secret to succeeding in your work is abiding in Christ."

Paul departed then, and I would never see him again as a free man.

Within days of my mentor's leaving, I felt overwhelmed by responsibilities. Serving as a pastor is never easy, even in the best congregation. But when a church suffers under the attacks of false doctrine, a lack of love, legalism, troublemaking, and materialism as we did in Ephesus, the ministry can be grueling. It wasn't long before I forgot to make time for Shayna. Our upcoming wedding was the furthest thing from my mind. I'd never imagined getting married without Paul there to officiate.

Shayna sensed my restlessness and withdrawal from her, finally grabbing me by the hand one day after our church gathering. "Timothy," she said, "you have been downhearted ever since Paul left."

"I'm just feeling overwhelmed," I admitted. "I like to think I can handle most things, but lately I find myself worrying."

"Your 'help comes from the LORD, who made heaven and earth,'"[262] she quoted the psalmist in her sweet, gentle voice. "Look to God, Tim. He will help you. Don't try to fight life's battles in your own power; you'll only grow discouraged. Look to God; He will strengthen you. With His help you will lead this church forward."

Shayna gave me much to think about. As I pondered her words, I realized that, unlike Paul, I didn't have physical eye problems; I could see fine, but I tended to focus on the negative. Over and over again, I allowed myself to replay mentally my many moments of frustration. As I did, I inevitably grew angry or depressed. *The key to joy is to focus on God,* I reminded myself. I must dwell on His goodness and nearness.

As the day of our wedding drew near, Shayna and I began to pray together daily. We would sit facing each other, knee-to-knee, holding hands as we interceded for everyone in the church and the local government,[263] often even asking for the Lord's blessing on our future together. Shayna and I also organized prayer meetings and invited as many as we could to join us.[264] Together we prayed for everyone, friend and foe alike. And we asked God to grant our church love, holiness, and sound doctrine, thanking Him that we were qualified to share in the Lord's inheritance because of our union with the Lord, because we were seated in heaven with Christ.

Almost overnight, the ministry in Ephesus began to improve. The fellowship among us grew sweeter, and the doctrine to which we held became more pure in our minds. I slowly started to feel much better about my assignment, praying in Jesus' name for answers—just as Paul had taught. Often, I found that the Lord's responses were accompanied by a renewal of joy in my heart.[265] Those days became some of the best of my life.

At the end of one very long Sunday, I sat down, leaned my head back, closed my eyes, and thanked the Lord for the good things He was doing in Ephesus. But the very next day my pastoral ministry ground to a sudden stop.

Grow as a Disciple:

Paul told Timothy to appreciate his union with Christ and to boldly claim his divine inheritance as a coheir. What is a Christian's divine inheritance? _____

_____

Circle the words that describe your position in Christ.

estranged, broken

distant, royal

intimate, wealthy

enduring, uncertain

What internal shifts must you make before you start praying like a child of the King? _____

_____

Should Christians pray with boldness or timidity? Why?

_____

_____

Memory Verse:

Commit to memory one of these verses: Galatians 4:7 or Hebrews 4:16. Write here for practice. _____

_____

_____

Prepare to Disciple Others:

A new Christian approaches you and asks for advice on how to pray. What will you say? _____

_____

_____

Chapter 12

DISCOVERING CHRIST'S RIGHTEOUSNESS

A.D. 66

The week of my wedding arrived, and with its dawn came Tychicus, an old friend from Rome. Though I greeted him warmly, he seemed agitated and refused to meet my eyes. Without saying a word, he handed me a letter from Paul. I'd heard little from him since his departure months ago, so Tychicus's odd behavior left me feeling unsettled.

"What is it?" I asked, fearful of what I might find inside the scroll. "Tell me, Tychicus. How does Paul fare?"

The middle-aged man sighed and said, "You've surely heard Emperor Nero's men started the fire in Rome. Numerous witnesses saw soldiers run from building to building, leaving destruction behind. Rumor has it that he intended to clear space for some grandiose plan of urban renewal. But the fire raged throughout Rome for almost a week. It got completely out of hand."

I'd heard about the fire. My stomach sank. "Was Paul harmed?"

"He wasn't harmed in the blaze, no."

My shoulders sagged in relief. I tried not to notice that Tychicus's face was still set in a grim expression.

"When public sentiment started to turn against the emperor," he continued, "Nero looked for a scapegoat. He blamed the fire on us, the Christians! A violent season of persecution has erupted against the church there, Timothy. They've arrested Paul." I heard a sob in his voice. "The conditions of his imprisonment are harsh." Tychicus looked into my eyes, his sorrow evident. "The poor man has been sentenced to death."

My breath caught, and I struggled to keep listening as Tychicus went on to say that Paul was cold and wet all the time. "With winter approaching, the living conditions are growing unbearable.[266] I expect this will be the last letter he'll ever write."

Quickly I broke the scroll's seal, scanning its contents. The words were fairly brief, more resigned than I'd ever known their writer to be. "This doesn't sound like the Paul I know." I'd come to expect a positive and strong outlook from the apostle, but in the letter he seemed accepting of death's sure approach.

"Will you go to him?" Tychicus asked. His words echoed the plea Paul had made in his missive.[267] "He's more or less deserted in Rome now. I wouldn't have left him, but he sent me here to take up the Ephesian pastorate in your stead."[268]

My head began to swim, my heart torn between helping my beloved friend or carrying on with the wedding that was only days away. "But I'm getting married in just a few days," I said.

"He may not have much longer than that," Tychicus replied.

Just then my soon-to-be wife stepped into the courtyard where we stood talking. I looked up glumly at Tychicus even as my happy bride linked her arm in mine.

I quickly introduced the two, and Tychicus did an admirable job of hiding his emotions as he chatted pleasantly with Shayna, clearly giving me time to think about what he'd said. I kept mulling over Paul's words, 'Do your utmost to come before winter.'[269] Autumn was drawing quickly to a close. Paul needed help right away.

"I'll go," I suddenly announced without preamble. Tychicus smiled, clearly relieved.

"Go? Go where?" Shayna asked, her beautiful eyes wide.

Tychicus excused himself, muttering something about how he would come by later with more details—which I would soon learn was simply a warning that being associated with Paul could be deadly. I was left to explain to Shayna that our wedding would have to be postponed.

The conversation did not go well. At the news, my lovely bride grieved like her heart was broken. I knew she respected and cared for Paul and her words of sympathy were sincere. But I hadn't counted on her charging me with abandonment and being completely opposed to my "hurrying away" without "marrying her first." Her words stung.

"Tim, we've waited years for our day," she cried, apparently forgetting that the neighbors could hear the outburst and liked nothing better than to discuss the goings-on between young couples. "I've practically become an old maid waiting for you! How can you just leave me like this? Why not take me along? We'll move the date up."

"It's not safe," I said, frustrated when she turned her back on me.

I reached for her, and she let me draw her closer, though remaining stiff. "I will be back, Shayna," I said, wishing I could give her a kiss to prove it but not wanting to give the neighbors more to talk about. "We will just have to delay the wedding a little bit. Here, read the letter for yourself." I handed it to her. "If Paul had anyone else to help him, I wouldn't go. He *needs* me."[270]

Her ruby lips quivered as she took the scroll and skimmed it, just as skilled at reading as was her mother, Priscilla. When she finished, she handed it back to me, sniffed daintily, and said, "You are right. You must go to him."

Relieved, I kissed her cheek lightly, thanked her enthusiastically, and moved to go pack my things. But my heart sank when I heard her next words: "I'm weary of delays, Tim. I may not be here when you get back."

I paused, swallowed hard, and then kept walking. *Surely her words are an empty threat,* I told myself. *She's only disappointed.*

The next morning I left Ephesus long before sunrise, knowing I couldn't stand to see further frustration in the faces of Shayna and her family. They'd spent much income and time planning an event that would be postponed indefinitely, and while everyone agreed that I was doing the right thing, no one liked my choice. Disheartened, I walked at a brisk pace and traveled several miles by the light of a full moon before I heard the first rooster crow. After that I started jogging, talking to the Lord about my own frustrations and fears.

In his letter, Paul asked me to bring John Mark too,[271] so I headed toward Colossae to fetch him. This required a quick race up the river to find him before we could begin the journey to Rome. I thought about what I remembered of Mark as I traveled, amazed at how the one-time missionary drop out had gone on to be further discipled by both Paul and Peter,[272] the latter of whom had actually walked alongside Christ and witnessed His miracles. Then, drawing from his lengthy conversations with Peter, Mark penned the first Gospel, a narrative that bears his name.

Mark seemed grateful to have been asked to accompany me. As per Paul's instructions, we stopped by Troas to pick up a cloak, books, and scrolls that Paul had left there.

When we finally arrived in Rome, our old friend Dr. Luke got word of our arrival and met us, not with warmth but with a warning. "Timothy, the situation is not the same as when you were here last. The political climate has dramatically changed. Nowadays Christians suffer persecution. If you go see Paul, you risk your life!"

"Is that why you and the others stay away?" I asked, feeling a bit of the old anger that had so long ruled me.

Luke looked sad but not ashamed. "Paul would be the first tell you that I go to him as often as I can,[273] but I'm an old man now. There's little I can do. Paul doesn't realize how dangerous it has become outside his pit."

"Forgive me," I said, wondering at his choice of words. "I know how you love him, and Paul did write that you were with him. Tell us, how can we help?"

The physician's brow creased. "The Romans moved Paul to the

Tullianum, an abandoned cistern, and this means that unless there is a miracle soon, Paul will be executed any day now. I know he asked you to bring his cloak and some other supplies. Likely the best thing you can do for him is to make that delivery."

I felt my throat tighten, and I noticed tears welling in the eyes of both my brothers in the Lord. Very soon our dear friend would be going to meet Jesus face-to-face. While that in itself was a beautiful thing, we would miss him deeply.

The next day, John Mark and I walked through the streets of Rome. Much of it was burned, dirty, and broken. The air was still heavy with ash. We passed the Circus Maximus where I once dreamed of racing chariots. We wove our way through markets and crowds of people. Finally, up ahead we spotted the Roman Forum; we knew we would find the prison in there.

Luke had warned us that Paul's accommodations were far worse than any we'd ever seen. Like the prophet Jeremiah of old, he'd been confined in little more than a hole in the ground.[274] As we entered the building, which was nice enough from the outside, the prison officials said Paul could only have one visitor a day. Mark waited. I followed the guards. To my astonishment, they led me to a literal hole in the stone floor. With their help, I soon dangled down a rope, descending about ten feet into the dark cavern. The only light came from the guard's torch above me.

Nothing could have prepared me for what I experienced once my feet found the floor. Within those walls was the most fearsome stench imaginable! The rock prison felt cold and very damp. Though I couldn't see very well, I could perceive I was standing in a small round room with a low ceiling. Over in the shadows, something moved. A rat let out a screech and scurried across my sandals.

I gasped.

"Who's there?" asked a raspy voice, achingly familiar yet drastically changed.

I soon realized that the large thing that had moved in the darkness was Paul. When I called out my name, I heard him push himself to his feet and shuffle my way. "My son!" he cried when he reached me, and I hugged him in spite of the filth surely clinging to his ragged garments. With my arms around Paul, I found new reason to be alarmed. Every rib protruded—his form so gaunt I could barely reconcile that the man I held was once the robust apostle who marched across the countryside proclaiming Jesus and firmly putting troublemakers like Nicolas DoM in their place. I could hardly believe the frail old man before me was Paul. He was so cold and clammy that I knew he was ill.

"I brought your cloak," I announced, swinging my pack off my shoulder and taking care not to let it touch the floor.

Paul sighed with pleasure as I helped him put on the woolen garment. "Warmth," he said. "How I've missed it." He folded his arms, and briskly rubbed them with his hands. "Did you have difficulty finding me?"

"No," I assured him. "Luke pointed me here—thanks to Onesiphorus. I'm told he's the one who first found you'd been moved."[275]

"I loved Onesiphorus," Paul said, his voice soft and eerily distant, realizing that particular friend had failed to return only because of his own demise. "My chains never embarrassed him, unlike the others who have all abandoned me."[276]

"Luke and I haven't abandoned you," I reminded him, "and John Mark is up above. He plans to come tomorrow. They let only one of us come down today."

"John Mark," he said, "I would so like to see him!"

Encouraged by his brightening tone I added, "Everything will be fine. You'll see. Somehow we'll find a way to get you out of here."

Paul grabbed for my arm, his bent fingers cold against my wrist. "No, dear one, you mustn't try to free me. The time of my departure is near. I am already being poured out as a drink offering."[277]

Somewhere in the room water dripped. Slowly. Steadily. I knew what Paul said was true. Changing the subject seemed the only way to escape my sadness. I reached again for my bag. "Your books and parchments are here, friend. Do you have a ledge where I can store them?"

"Thank you, my son," Paul replied, "but no. I will not need them now. Give the books to John Mark. The parchments I want you to have. They belong to you."

As I stood there in the cistern shaft with the vellum in my hand and the stink of despair heavy in the air, I didn't know what to say. Deep down I knew I'd never see Paul again—at least not until I too stepped into eternity. He seemed to sense my emotions and patted my arm gently. "Master this material," he said. "Teach these principles to faithful people. Insist your students share these teachings with others. These truths must be passed from generation to generation."

"I'll do it," I replied.

Suddenly the flickering light above us got brighter, the guard leaning over the hole with his torch to announce our time was nearly up.

I sent up a shout that I understood, swallowed hard, and this time I reached for my friend's hand. "Teach me one more lesson, Paul... please."

The old apostle squeezed my fingers and smiled so brightly I could see it clearly in the dim light. He took a deep breath, cleared his throat, and—in spite of his rusty voice and hushed volume—spoke with as much passion and authority as ever. "Never forget the difference between performance and position, Timothy. Your performance as a minister of the gospel, what you do, has been exemplary."

"Except for a few times I'd rather forget about," I admitted, cringing over the time I'd nearly attacked Maximus.

"You have a rare quality about you: you care about people,"[278] he continued, as if he hadn't heard me. "Over and over again, you have proven your worth as a worker for Christ's church. Through good times and bad you have labored at my side, just like a son beside his father.[279] You have done more for the Lord in your brief lifetime than most men much older than you would care to attempt." He paused to catch his breath. "But I want you to always remember that your position as the Lord's chosen vessel is more important than anything you can do. You reign with Christ. You live in Christ, seated at the Father's right hand. Hidden in Christ,[280] then, you are acceptable to God—whether you excel in the world's eyes or not. In the Father's eyes you are accepted and loved just for who you are—because who you are is in and with Christ. God sees you as righteous, blameless, and approved."[281]

"Even when I don't feel particularly righteous?" I asked, knowing the answer, yet needing to hear my mentor's affirmation once more.

"Feelings have nothing to do with your position in Christ," my friend assured me, love evident in his weakened voice. "If there are sins in your life, confess and forsake them,[282] but if you are not aware of any sins, rest in the reality of your righteous position. Because you reign in Christ, you can and must enjoy *His* righteousness."

Before I could reply, another bright bit of light shone down from above. The guard stuck his head down through the opening above us. "Time's up. You gotta get outta there."

I sent up an acknowledgement and stepped back into the loop of rope that the guards used to haul visitors in and out, feeling a moment of panic. *Will I ever see Paul again?* I wondered.

My beloved mentor, sensing my sadness, wrapped his gnarled fingers around my forearms and squeezed gently. He caught my gaze and held it with his own. "To be absent from the body is to be present with the Lord,"[283] he said with conviction. "This is not good-bye, Timothy. This is only until we meet again."

Grow as a Disciple:

Paul helped Timothy understand that because of his position in Christ he was completely righteous. Are you in Christ? What does that mean? _____

_____

What is the difference between performance-based righteousness and positional righteousness? _____

_____

_____

Is the righteousness of God achieved through effort or faith? Explain your answer. _____

_____

_____

How would your life be different if you lived in the reality that God accepts you completely? _____

_____

_____

Memory Verse:

Select either Romans 8:1 or 2 Corinthians 5:21 to commit to memory. Write here for practice. _____

_____

_____

Prepare to Disciple Others:

If you were counseling a despondent Christian who said, "I'm no good," what would you say? _____

_____

_____

Chapter 13

DISCIPLESHIP MULTIPLIED

A.D. 66

That very afternoon John Mark and I called a secret meeting in the home of a local believer. We intended to show Paul's scrolls and parchments to those few brave enough to attend and to encourage them in the faith. But no sooner than we had sung an opening hymn the door flew open, and five fierce Roman guards entered the tiny house, swords drawn. Within moments we were all under arrest for the crime of confessing Jesus as Lord. In other words, we were worshiping someone other than Caesar, and that was strictly forbidden. Likely, many believed, all such persons were direct accessories behind the great fire of Rome.

Within the hour John Mark and I sat in a prison cell together, our valuables—including the precious documents—confiscated. Whereas I'd felt the guards who stood watch over Paul's cistern turned a deaf ear to the goings-on between him and his visitors, our guards demanded silence and were thoroughly hostile toward the faith. The more I thought about it, the more I wondered whether one of Paul's guards had followed John Mark and me once we left our friend. It was likely one of them had been an informant.

On our second day in the prison, when it seemed the sour-faced guards were engaged in conversation and not paying any attention to us, I began to hum a tune of praise. I thought I was quiet about it, but even as the first notes vibrated in my throat, the meanest of the jailers was upon me. He grabbed me by the hair, called me several choice names, and then gave me a kick in the side that took my breath away. "Stupid Christian," he sneered, talking to the other guard who watched over us with him. "They're all alike."

The second soldier laughed as if my mistreatment were a great joke. Then he began to tell stories of how other Christians he'd seen had been disposed of in grisly ways: some were even fed to wild beasts in the Colosseum. When I heard him speak of "the one they call Paul" who was rumored to "refuse to stay dead," my gaze locked with John Mark's. The guard casually mentioned that a friend of his had walked the old man down the Ostian Road and outside of town. "Marcus personally cut his head clean off," he bragged, as if he was proud of his acquaintance for finally ridding the world of the famed follower of Jesus.

John Mark looked as if he might be sick at any moment, and tears welled up in my eyes at the news. I gasped for air, staring at the wall in disbelief. Paul, my spiritual father, the one who had taught me so much, was gone. Though John Mark and I knew Paul had finished his race and now stood in the Lord's presence, our grief threatened to crush us. It was such an awful end for such a wonderful man. How I hoped Paul's suffering had been brief.

Three days later, Luke and some other Christians were able to get us out of jail. Most of our things were returned, and we were free.

The news was not all good, however. Not only was the church aware of Paul's demise. The fisherman turned apostle Peter, too, had lost his life. The Romans crucified him upside down. Terrible persecution was becoming common in Rome, and it seemed fleeing the city quickly was the wisest thing to do if I hoped to see Shayna again.

That very afternoon I packed, anxious to get back to Ephesus and eager to distance myself from the place of bad memories. As I readied my supplies, I took special care with the parchment Paul had given me only days earlier. I gave it one last look before strapping it to my middle where it would hide under my clothing:

Whether he had intended it as an outline of a letter or perhaps meant to turn it into a sequel for the book of Romans, the document systematized his views on sanctification beautifully. It also bore witness to the many times when I'd learned at Paul's side, taking in truths such as Christ was crucified for me, and I am crucified in Christ. Christ reigns in me, and I reign in Christ. It reminded me of all I'd grasped about following the Lord's guidance, finding reconciliation, focusing on His love, and adopting the attitude of Jesus. It helped me recall what I knew of Christ's power, hope, and authority—all particularly valuable aids given the insecurity and turmoil the church in Rome faced. It helped me find serenity in Him, trusting that, in the Lord, we as a church already had liberty and victory. No matter how bad things might grow, we could trust in our inheritance with Christ, and we could continue to live in His righteousness. One day, no matter how bleak things seemed, He would set all things right.

"The church in Ephesus needs to see this," I said to Luke as I packed, patting the document. He sat on a bench in the corner of the rented room John Mark and I had shared with him briefly, watching me tie the parchment to my midsection. I suspected he was a little sad Paul had not left such a fine gift to him, even more so to know what had happened to our mutual friend.

"Are you certain you won't stay here, Timothy?" he asked. "With both Paul and Peter gone now, our church here in Rome is really going to need a good man. You know the Word as well as anyone, and we must have leadership."

The church positioned in the capitol of the Roman Empire had great potential for kingdom impact—even in the face of persecution. Were the threat to pass, in fact, the man who pastored in Rome might reasonably expect riches and fame to one day surround him. Still, I could not accept. "I appreciate the offer, Luke," I said, knowing my elderly friend was far too busy with his medical duties to consider filling the role. "But I have got to get back to Shayna. In Ephesus there's a wedding waiting for a bridegroom."

Luke and I parted ways, and it occurred to me as we drew apart that

I might not see him again in my lifetime either. The first generation of Christ-followers was quickly dying off—whether from martyrdom or simply old age. How important, then, that younger men like John Mark and myself not grow complacent in sharing all we knew about Jesus. Our time, too, might prove short.

An hour later I said a hasty good-bye to John Mark and headed out. I made quick progress, though even that pace seemed too slow when I considered my future with Shayna. By the time I reached Macedonia, I'd decided to take an untried shortcut. But when I got off the main road, the trail became narrow and dark. The forest was thick, and the weeds were high. I quickly grew disoriented.

For a moment I thought I heard an animal to my left, and I paused to get my bearings. Undoubtedly large creatures lived in the area, and I didn't want to become one's meal. But when the rustling got closer, I tensed and reached for my knife. I'd not quite worked it out of its scabbard when something dove out of the greenery and shoved me to the ground. Grunting in surprise, I panicked when the thing landed on top of me. For a moment, I was certain it was a bear. But when the hairy creature wrestled my knife from me and called me a "low-down poaching thief," I realized my attacker was a local farmer. Lately he'd lost several swine to strangers like me, he growled, and he was ready for revenge.

In no time, in spite of my protests, I was soundly beaten and thrown into the local jailhouse. I rotted in that cell, no one knowing my location or whether I was even alive. By the end of my first year there I'd decided that my bride had surely given herself to another. I hoped with all my heart she hadn't married the one visitor I'd had.

About a month after the start of my incarceration, a visitor came to the jail to meet with his friend, the man who ran the prison. When he was given a tour of the facility, the visitor stopped in front of my cell. Completely disheartened by that time, I lay on the floor, not even looking up to see who'd come by. I heard the two whispering about something and the man in charge of the place excused himself. After he walked away, I could feel the visitor's eyes on me.

Several minutes passed before he finally spoke. "My, my, my, how the mighty have fallen," hissed an oily voice that I recognized all too well. Nicolas DoM, of all people, had stumbled upon me.

I scrambled to my feet as soon as I heard him. Our eyes locked, and the contempt in his reminded me I was just as dirty and unkempt as he was clean and neat. "Yes, I've fallen into unfortunate circumstances," I said. "But it's all just a misunderstanding."

Nicolas sneered, clearly disbelieving me and not willing to use his influence with the jail owner on my behalf. Still, since no one else knew what had become of me, I had to try. "Nicolas, please, help me. No one knows I'm here. Will you please get word to Aquila, tentmaker of Ephesus? Tell him I'm trapped in here. You don't even have to go there. Just send him a letter. The jailer won't allow me to."

Nicolas thought for a moment, and I didn't like the look on his face when his eyes narrowed. "Ephesus, you say? Isn't that the very place where you and Paul," he spit the name, "chose to make a fool of me?"

"I am sorry if we embarrassed you," I said.

His face turned red and his gaze menacing. "I am *never* embarrassed, only annoyed." He pursed his lips, and an odd smile suddenly claimed his features. "But I suppose I do have an account to settle with you. It seems I never did make good on my promise to slit your throat."

I swallowed.

"I seem to remember," he said smoothly, "having heard of a certain young woman in Ephesus whose groom deserted her on the eve of their wedding. Shayna, I believe is her name." He eyed me, gauging the reaction I was trying to hide. Then his voice turned lecherous. "I've often thought of this Shayna, for they say she is young, lovely, and *very* lonely. It could be time that I go and claim the poor little deserted dove as my own." He smirked. "Tell me, Timothy, what do you think?"

It was all I could do not to spit in his face and shout that he was old enough to be her father, so I turned my back to him, walked a few paces away, and sat down. Nothing I could say would stop him. Prayer and Shayna's good sense were my only hope.

Nicolas walked away, chuckling in a way that made me cringe. I heard nothing from him, my friends in Ephesus, or anyone else save my captors for many, many months.

In the second year of my imprisonment I grew terribly sick. Whether poisoned by a mosquito's bite or the contaminated food I was sometimes served, I fell under the effects of chills, nausea, vomiting, and night sweats until every drop of strength was sapped from me. I expected and received no sympathy from the jailer, but he did throw me a dirty blanket covered with animal hair. That filthy item was my only physical comfort as I waited for death.

My dreams grew vivid as I began to lose my grip on life. One night it seemed I saw Paul enter my cell. For a long time he simply looked at me before he said, "All who desire to live godly in Christ Jesus will suffer persecution."[284] His image vanished as quickly from my dreams as it had arrived.

Days later my fever broke, and I was surprised to wake up both alive and in the presence of another prisoner: for many months I'd been alone most of the time. "Who are you?" I managed to ask, propping my emaciated body up against the wall so I could sit and speak with him.

"I am Amnon," he answered. He was a small man with narrow shoulders, and both his bare arms and chest were covered with tattoos. "For many days I've taken care of you."

I thanked him sincerely, realizing he must have used his own scant rations—and perhaps some medicinal herbs smuggled in past the jailer—to help me. "Why did they put you in here?" I asked. "What did you do?"

He replied that his father was a ship's physician who'd run into trouble and he was guiltless of any crime worthy of prison; I believed him. In the coming days, Amnon and I became friends, quickly sharing our secrets. His plan, he said, was to get out of jail with bribe money his wife and brother were gathering. "It's the only way out of this corrupt place," he insisted. As long as I'd been there, I decided he was probably right on that point too.

About a week after my fever broke, I'd gained the strength to think and teach clearly. It was time to share about Jesus with Amnon, rather than only mentioning Him in passing as I'd done up to then. Paul's parchment, now limp and dirty but still strapped to my thin body, became the visual I produced and used to tell Amnon about Christ's death, resurrection, and love.

My tattooed cellmate seemed receptive to my message, though he hesitated to join with the Christian group so often persecuted. I watched him wrestle with the dilemma for days before he finally asked me how I could follow a Christ who allowed me and His other followers to suffer so. Immediately, Paul's words from my dream came to mind.

I shared them, and then told Amnon about Paul, my mentor who had long suffered for the gospel because he knew that his message was straight from the Lord and was essential for giving the world hope. I told him of the times Paul was beaten, shipwrecked, falsely accused, imprisoned, and mistreated, yet always remained faithful to Christ. "I know it sounds incredible," I admitted, "but when I was a boy I thought I'd find joy and fulfillment in adventure. Maybe it would come through seeing the world. But in my years alongside Paul I discovered that true joy comes from the grace of Jesus Christ,[285] not from favorable circumstances. Seasons of hardship come and go, good times rise and fall, but the joy from the Lord outshines them all—even today."

"So you'll happily identify with this Christ," Amnon said, "even when others mistreat you for it?"

I smiled sadly, remembering Paul's end. "I will," I said. "But it isn't such a hard trade."

His mouth fell open. "How can you say that, man? Look at yourself! You're a mess. Just look at what your god has done for you."

"*Everyone* will suffer to some extent in life," I replied, refusing to look down at my tattered clothes. "Yet suffering with Christ has a point, a promised end. Just as important, when we belong to Jesus, we find new power for dealing with life's challenges." I smiled, my dry skin stretching taut with the effort. "By cultivating a relationship with Jesus we exchange loneliness for His love, the shame over our sins for reconciliation with our Creator, despair over the hard times for hope that better days are ahead, confusion for His guidance, selfishness for His attitude of love for others, weakness for His power, discontentment for the serenity He offers, rule-keeping for liberty in Christ, fear for trust in His ultimate authority, and rejection for His righteousness. So joy," I finished, "flows from attitude, not location. I'd much rather stand with Christ than try to do life without Him."

A few days later, Amnon's wife visited the jail with the bribe money in hand. Amnon had accepted Christ as Savior just that morning, and I wished I could go with him to help him grow in his faith. "I want you to take this parchment," I said, handing him Paul's scroll just before his release. "You've heard me teach from this many times, and you know what it means to me. Please, memorize the truth here and seek to connect with other believers. After you have mastered this, you must share it."

Once again alone, I faced my greatest test. Would the exchanged life with Christ really be a source of supernatural joy? Determined, I dropped to my knees, spread my arms wide like a flower spreading its petals to the sun, and thanked God for Christ's sufficiency. Then I began to sing. I praised God that way every day for months, learning better than ever that God was not just all I had, He is everything I need.

Soon my captor started calling me "the Singing Ephesian." The weeks dragged on as my beard grew long and my clothes more ragged. During the long, dark nights, I thought of my grandmother and our final moments together. I rehearsed the Royal Prayer she taught me: "When I am afraid, I will trust in You.[286] When I am lonely, I will trust in You. When I cannot see tomorrow, I will trust in You." Each new morning, I looked up to God in faith, like a baby bird in the nest, expecting necessary provision and receiving just what I needed to endure another day of solitude.

My release came on a Tuesday. After holding me for three years on nothing more than the word of an irritable farmer, the jailer found that his own gambling debts had mounted past his ability to repay. He was killed for his crimes, and the new jailer—disgusted by the story I shared about the circumstances of my imprisonment—let me go. "Besides," he said, "your Christian praise songs make me feel uncomfortable." Then he suggested that I bathe and put on the spare clothing he'd brought me before I attempted to rejoin the world.

I shouted with joy when he released me from jail[287] after filling me with the best meal I'd eaten in months, not even caring when my ivory-handled dagger could not be found. I stepped out into the sunshine, wishing I could kick up my heels like a spring calf yet knowing my renewed energy was better spent as the jailer had suggested. As I made tracks to the nearest river for a good bath, I realized all my earthly goods were gone and my strength was not what it once was. Still, I felt I could return to Ephesus as a rich man. The fresh air felt clean, and the honeysuckle blooms smelled sweet as new wine. Yellow daffodils sprouted forth from the moist soil, and robins flitted across the meadow in search of earthworms. Freedom felt fantastic.

As I journeyed toward Ephesus, I thought of two things: Shayna and the church I'd long ago left in Tychicus's hands. As much as it pained me to admit it, I expected Shayna had married; surely I'd find her with a child on her hip. The church, I hoped, had fared well in the years of my absence. I felt they would benefit from news of my reappearance and would welcome me back into the flock as a long-lost brother if not as their pastor. Still, there was so much material I wanted to share to help the congregation mature in the faith. I knew Paul's lessons about identification with Christ had never been only for introspection but rather were tools meant to give those I'd meet inspiration for missions, ministry, and disciple-making.

Once in Ephesus, I went straight to Priscilla and Aquila's house. I dropped my walking stick at their front door and knocked. Only a moment later, Priscilla appeared. A little older yet much the same as I remembered her, she let out a squeal, hugged my neck, and began to weep with joy. She let go of me only long enough to shout up the steps leading to the roof. "Come, daughter! Come, Aquila! See what the Lord has brought us this day!"

Only moments later, Shayna was in my arms and Aquila was slapping me on the back. "I knew you'd come! I just knew you'd come back!" my fiancé said through happy tears. The enthusiastic greeting was all I needed to assure me she'd waited for me.

I spent the evening telling the story of my trip to Rome and my unfortunate stay in Macedonia, leaving out the part about Nicolas DoM. For several weeks, I worked to regain my strength through good food and basic chores. Then, less than a month after my return, Shayna and I married.

That same week Paul's friend Onesimus handed leadership of the local congregation back to me. "She's all yours, Saint Timothy," said the runaway-slave-turned-preacher who'd replaced Tychicus as bishop to our church when I failed to reappear within that first year.

To my relief, the people of Ephesus were quick to remember and embrace me. New converts and migrants soon joined our work, family members among them. After Mother went on to glory, my sister Hitty and her husband left Lystra specifically to help our church. The years had mellowed her for the better. She was far less bossy and soon began leading afternoon Scripture studies for the women in the various churches around Ephesus. The Lord had calmed both our tempers as we matured spiritually, and we got along well.

I kept my promise to Paul, faithfully sharing his teachings and working to spread the good news of Christ. Like leaven, the gospel made its way throughout our province. Even under the ever-present threat of persecution and in spite of the terrible things going on in Jerusalem, congregations thrived in Troas, Colossae, Hierapolis, Laodicea, Smyrna, Pergamos, Thyatira, Sardis, and Philadelphia.[288] New house churches continued to spring up everywhere[289] too, and in time I even received news that Amnon had not only learned and shared the message on Paul's parchment. He'd become a missionary to his entire region. The gospel was fast making its way to the ends of the earth.

Stories like Amnon's grew increasingly common as those new to Christ chose to grow in Him, taking their testimonies and their knowledge of Scripture to others who'd never heard the good news and encouraging those still weak in the faith. As those new believers matured, they too would seek to reach out according to that same pattern because only through this cycle would Christ's Great Commission be fulfilled: "Go therefore," He'd said, "and make disciples of all the nations."[290] The Lord does not desire mere converts to Christianity: He wants followers fully devoted to applying His Word and serving Him.

Jesus Christ came to answer life's most basic questions: Are we loved? Is there hope? Can we be forgiven? With His cross and crown, He brought the resounding answer: "Yes!"

But how will the world know, unless they are told? And how will new Christians grow unless they are shown?

Grow as a Disciple:

While in prison Timothy had plenty of time to reflect on Paul's teachings about victorious Christian living. Of all the things taught in this book, what has been the most meaningful to you? Why? _____

_____

Whom would you identify as your "Paul"? Who has mentored you in the faith? _____

_____

Consider the trials and persecutions faced by the early church fathers and many others since. What does their sacrifice and determination in the face of such dangers tell you about the necessity of spreading God's Word? _____

_____

_____

Memory Verse:

Select either Colossians 1:28 or 2 Timothy 2:2 to commit to memory. Write here for practice. _____

_____

_____

Prepare to Disciple Others:

Think about and list the younger or less mature Christians you know. Those people have the potential of becoming your next Timothy. Select one person from your list. How might you invest in him this week? (Treating him to coffee and giving him a copy of this book might be a good place to start.) _____

_____

_____

EPILOGUE

According to church tradition, Timothy suffered a martyr's fate in Ephesus on January 22, 97. On a feast day for the goddess Artemis, a raucous crowd of worshipers paraded through the city. When Timothy tried to stop their pagan procession by proclaiming the gospel of Jesus Christ, the angry mob beat the old man, dragged him through the streets, and then stoned him to death.

In the fourth century, Constantine transferred the bones of Timothy to Constantinople. With that move Timothy finally made it to the big city he dreamed of seeing as a teenage boy. Timothy's remains were placed in The Church of the Holy Apostles, alongside those of Luke the physician and Andrew, one of the twelve disciples who had traveled with Christ.

Each January, various churches—especially those among Roman Catholic, Lutheran, Episcopalian, and Eastern Orthodox denominations—celebrate the life of Timothy with a feast day in his honor. This commemorates the day angels carried Timothy to heaven. Although Timothy's physical life is over, his memory remains, and his legacy continues to this very hour.

How to Know You Are a Christian

"Christian" is a term that identifies those who have turned away from sin and self-righteousness and placed their faith in Jesus Christ, inviting the Lord to work in their lives. Christians a) acknowledge their sin, admitting that because of personal disobedience they have fallen short of the glory of God; b) believe in Jesus, putting faith in His vicarious death, burial, and resurrection; and c) call on the Lord, repenting of their sin and asking Him to forgive and save them.

Perhaps long ago you followed those steps above, even praying a public prayer in a church service, but today—months or even years later—you don't feel much different than you did before. It's important to realize that the absence of feelings does not mean you are unsaved. In fact, a simple test will help you know whether or not you are saved.

John, the beloved apostle, wrote, "These things I have written to you who believe in the name of the Son of God, *that you may know that you have eternal life*" (1 John 5:13, emphasis mine). To what "things" did he refer? Throughout the book of 1 John, he puts forth a four-question test to help readers verify their salvation:

1. Do you acknowledge and confess that Jesus is the only Savior? (1 John 2:23; 4:15; 5:1)

2. Does the Holy Spirit abide within you? (1 John 3:24; 4:13)

3. Do you love God's people? (1 John 2:10; 3:14; 4:7)

4. Is it your desire to obey God's commands and avoid sin? (1 John 2:3; 3:6,9; 5:18)

If you answered the above questions positively, no matter how you feel, you can be sure of your salvation. Once you have scripturally established that you are saved, you need to grow in your faith. Through reading God's book, the Holy Bible, and other sound resources such as *Discipleship Matters*; through prayer; and church involvement; as well as through a mentoring relationship like the one between Paul and Timothy, you can grow and mature in your faith.

ENDNOTES

PART ONE

Front Matter

i.　1 Tim. 6:11, "But you, O man of God."

ii.　2 Tim. 1:2, "To Timothy, a beloved son."

iii.　1 Tim. 1:2, "To Timothy, a true son in the faith."

iv.　Rom. 5:10, "For if when we were enemies we were reconciled to God through the death of His Son, much more, having been reconciled, *we shall be saved by His life* (author's emphasis)."

v.　2 Cor. 5:21, "For He made Him who knew no sin to be sin for us, that we might become the righteousness of God in Him."

vi.　Rom. 5:18, "Through one Man's righteous act *the free gift came* to all men, resulting in *justification* of life (author's emphasis)."

vii.　1 Thess. 5:23, "Now may the God of peace Himself *sanctify* you completely; and may your whole spirit, soul, and body be preserved blameless at the coming of our Lord Jesus Christ (author's emphasis)."

viii.　Matthew 28:19-20, "Go therefore and make disciples of all the nations, baptizing them in the name of the Father and of the Son and of the Holy Spirit, teaching them to observe all things that I have commanded you; and lo, I am with you always, even to the end of the age."

Chapter 1

1.　See Acts 14:8-18.

2.　Acts 14:19, "Then Jews from Antioch and Iconium came there; and having persuaded the multitudes, they stoned Paul and dragged him out of the city, supposing him to be dead."

3.　Acts 14:20, "When the disciples gathered around him, he rose up and went into the city."

4.　2 Cor. 12:2-4, "I know a man in Christ who fourteen years ago—whether in the body I do not know, or whether out of the body I do not know, God knows—such a one was caught up to the third heaven. And I know such a man—whether in the body or out of the body I do not know, God knows—how he was caught up into Paradise and heard inexpressible words, which it is not lawful for a man to utter."

5.　See Gen. 1—4.

6.   See 1 Cor. 2:14—3:4.

7.   2 Tim. 3:15, "From childhood you have known the Holy Scriptures, which are able to make you wise for salvation through faith which is in Christ Jesus."

8.   Acts 16:2, "He was well spoken of by the brethren who were at Lystra and Iconium."

9.   Acts 6:5, "And they chose Stephen, a man full of faith and the Holy Spirit, and Philip, Prochorus, Nicanor, Timon, Parmenas, and Nicolas, a proselyte from Antioch."

10. Psalm 1:1, "Blessed is the man who walks not in the counsel of the ungodly, nor stands in the path of sinners, nor sits in the seat of the scornful."

11. Acts 16:1, "A certain disciple was there, named Timothy, the son of a certain Jewish woman who believed, but his father was Greek."

12. Gal. 5:1, "Stand fast therefore in the liberty by which Christ has made us free, and do not be entangled again with a yoke of bondage."

13. Ps. 56:3, "Whenever I am afraid, I will trust in You."

14. 1 Tim. 4:14, "Do not neglect the gift that is in you, which was given to you by prophecy with the laying on of the hands of the eldership."

15. 2 Tim. 4:5, "Do the work of an evangelist, fulfill your ministry."

16. Ancient Byzantium is modern Istanbul. Over the millennia the city has had three names: Byzantium, Constantinople, and now Istanbul.

17. 1 Cor. 6:20, "For you were bought at a price; therefore glorify God in your body and in your spirit, which are God's."

18. Rom. 5:8, "God demonstrates His own love toward us, in that while we were still sinners, Christ died for us."

19. Rom. 8:38-39, "For I am persuaded that neither death nor life, nor angels nor principalities nor powers, nor things present nor things to come, nor height nor depth, nor any other created thing, shall be able to separate us from the love of God which is in Christ Jesus our Lord."

20. Isa. 54:10, ESV, "My steadfast love shall not depart from you."

21. Jer. 31:3, "I have loved you with an everlasting love."

22. Phil. 4:8, "Whatever things are true, whatever things are noble, whatever things are just, whatever things are pure, whatever things are lovely, whatever things are of good report, if there is any virtue and if there is anything praiseworthy—meditate on these things."

Chapter Two

23. Hab. 2:14, "For the earth will be filled with the knowledge of the glory of the Lord, as the water covers the sea."

24. Gal. 5:12, "I could wish that those who trouble you would even cut themselves off!"

25. Gal. 1:6-7, "I marvel that you are turning away so soon from Him who called you in the grace of Christ, to a different gospel, which is not another; but there are some who trouble you and want to pervert the gospel of Christ."

26. Gal. 5:1, "Stand fast therefore in the liberty by which Christ has made us free, and do not be entangled again with a yoke of bondage."

27. Acts 16:6-7, "When they had gone through Phrygia and the region of Galatia, they were forbidden by the Holy Spirit to preach the word in Asia. After they had come to Mysia, they tried to go into Bithynia, but the Spirit did not permit them."

28. Acts 16:8, "Passing by Mysia, they came down to Troas."

29. Acts. 16:9-10, "A vision appeared to Paul in the night. A man of Macedonia stood and pleaded with him, saying, 'Come over to Macedonia and help us.' Now after he had seen the vision, immediately we sought to go to Macedonia, concluding that the Lord had called us to preach the gospel to them."

30. Macedonia is still known as the gateway to Europe. Up to Paul's focus there, the gospel had been limited to Asia. Many historians credit Paul's heeding the Macedonian call with the spread of Christianity into Europe and the western world.

31. Acts 16:11, "Sailing from Troas, we ran a straight course to Samothrace, and the next day came to Neapolis."

32. Isa. 30:21, "Your ears shall hear a word behind you, saying, 'This is the way, walk in it.'"

33. John 10:4, "When he brings out his own sheep, he goes before them; and the sheep follow him, for *they know his voice* (author's emphasis)."

34. John 14:26, "But the Helper, the Holy Spirit, whom the Father will send in My name, He will teach you all things."

35. Rom. 8:6, "For to be carnally minded *is* death, but *to be spiritually minded is life and peace* (author's emphasis)."

36. Col. 3:15, "Let the peace of God rule in your hearts."

37. Jer. 17:9, "The heart is deceitful above all things, and desperately wicked; who can know it?"

38. Acts 13:13, "When Paul and his party set sail from Paphos, they came to Perga in Pamphylia; and John, departing from them, returned to Jerusalem."

Chapter Three

39. See Acts 16:16-21.

40. Acts 16:23, "And when they had laid many stripes on them, they threw them into prison, commanding the jailer to keep them securely."

41. See Acts 16:13-15.

42. Acts 16:26, "Suddenly there was a great earthquake, so that the foundations of the prison were shaken; and immediately all the doors were opened and everyone's chains were loosed."

43. Acts 16:28, "Paul called with a loud voice, saying, "Do yourself no harm, for we are all here."

44. Acts 16:30, "Sirs, what must I do to be saved?"

45. 1 John 1:9, "If we confess our sins, He is faithful and just to forgive us our sins and to cleanse us from all unrighteousness."

46. John 5:24, "He who hears My word and believes in Him who sent Me has everlasting life, and shall not come into judgment, but has passed from death into life."

47. Gal. 1:13 "I persecuted the church of God beyond measure and tried to destroy it."

48. Acts 9:4, "Then he fell to the ground, and heard a voice saying to him, 'Saul, Saul, why are you persecuting Me?'"

49. 1 Tim. 1:15, "This *is* a faithful saying and worthy of all acceptance, that Christ Jesus came into the world to save sinners, of whom I am chief."

50. Col. 1:21-22, "And you, who once were alienated and enemies in your mind by wicked works, yet now *He has reconciled* in the body of His flesh through death, to present you holy, and blameless, and above reproach in His sight (author's emphasis)."

51. Eph. 2:13, "But now in Christ Jesus you who once were far off have been brought near by the blood of Christ."

52. 2 Cor. 5:18, "Now all things are of God, who has reconciled us to Himself through Jesus Christ, and has given us the ministry of reconciliation."

53. Isa. 53:6, "All we like sheep have gone astray; we have turned, every one, to his own way; and *the Lord has laid on Him the iniquity of us all* (author's emphasis)."

54. Acts 16:30, "Sirs, what must I do to be saved?"

55. Rom. 1:16, "For I am not ashamed of the gospel of Christ, for it is the power of God to salvation for everyone who believes, for the Jew first and also for the Greek."

56. Rom. 3:10, "There is none righteous, no, not one."

57. Rom. 3:23, "All have sinned and fall short of the glory of God."

58. Rom. 6:23, "The wages of sin is death, but the gift of God is eternal life in Christ Jesus our Lord."

59. Rom. 5:8, "God demonstrates His own love toward us, in that while we were still sinners, Christ died for us."

60. Rom. 2:4, "Do you despise the riches of His goodness, forbearance, and longsuffering, not knowing that the goodness of God leads you to repentance?"

61. Rom. 10:9, "If you confess with your mouth the Lord Jesus and believe in your heart that God has raised Him from the dead, you will be saved."

62. Rom. 10:13, "Whoever calls on the name of the LORD shall be saved."

63. Eph. 2:8-9, "For by grace you have been saved through faith, and that not of yourselves; it is the gift of God, not of works, lest anyone should boast."

64. 2 Tim. 1:5; 3:15: "I call to remembrance the genuine faith that is in you, which dwelt first in your grandmother Lois and your mother Eunice, and I am persuaded is in you also…From childhood you have known the Holy Scriptures."

65. Isa. 1:18, "'Come now, and let us reason together,' says the Lord, 'though your sins are like scarlet, they shall be as white as snow; though they are red like crimson, they shall be as wool.'"

66. Mic. 7:19, "You will cast all our sins into the depths of the sea."

67. Jer. 31:34, "I will forgive their iniquity, and their sin I will remember no more."

68. Ps. 103:12, "As far as the east is from the west, so far has He removed our transgressions from us."

69. Acts 16:31, "So they said, 'Believe on the Lord Jesus Christ, and you will be saved, you and your household.'"

70. 2 Cor. 5:21, "He made Him who knew no sin to be sin for us, that we might become the righteousness of God in Him."

71. Eph. 4:32, "Be kind to one another, tenderhearted, *forgiving one another, even as God in Christ forgave you* (author's emphasis)."

72. Matt. 18:21-22, "Then Peter came to Him and said, 'Lord, how often shall my brother sin against me and I forgive him? Up to seven times?' Jesus said to him, 'I do not say to you, up to seven times, but up to seventy times seven.'"

73. Acts 16:34, "Now when he had brought them into his house, he set food before them; and he rejoiced, having believed in God with all his household."

Chapter Four

74. Acts 16:38-39, "They were afraid when they heard that they were Romans. Then they came and pleaded with them and brought them out, and asked them to depart from the city."

75. Acts 22:27-28, "The commander came and said to him, 'Tell me, are you a Roman?' He said, 'Yes.' The commander answered, 'With a large sum I obtained this citizenship.' And Paul said, 'But I was born a citizen.'"

76. Acts 16:40, "So they went out of the prison and entered the house of Lydia; and when they had seen the brethren, they encouraged them and departed."

77. Neh. 8:10, "Do not sorrow, for the joy of the LORD is your strength."

78. Gal. 5:22-23, "The fruit of the Spirit is love, joy, peace, longsuffering, kindness, goodness, faithfulness, gentleness, self-control. Against such there is no law."

79. John 7:37-39, "Jesus stood and cried out, saying, 'If anyone thirsts, let him come to Me and drink. He who believes in Me, as the Scripture has said, out of his heart will flow rivers of living water.' But this He spoke concerning the Spirit, whom those believing in Him would receive; for the Holy Spirit was not yet given, because Jesus was not yet glorified."

80. Lev. 11:44, "For I am the LORD your God. You shall therefore consecrate yourselves, and you shall be holy; for I am holy."

81. See Eph. 4:31—5:4.

82. Eph. 4:30, "Do not grieve the Holy Spirit of God, by whom you were sealed for the day of redemption."

83. 1 John 1:9, "If we confess our sins, He is faithful and just to forgive us *our* sins and to cleanse us from all unrighteousness."

84. Ps. 51:2, "Wash me thoroughly from iniquity, and cleanse me from my sin."

85. Rom. 12:1, "I beseech you therefore, brethren, by the mercies of God, that you *present your bodies a living sacrifice*, holy, acceptable to God, *which is* your reasonable service (author's emphasis)."

86. See Gal. 5:16-26.

87. See Col. 3:8-12.

88. Luke 11:13, "If you then, being evil, know how to give good gifts to your children, how much more will your heavenly Father give the Holy Spirit to those who ask Him!"

89. Matt. 5:41, "Whoever compels you to go one mile, go with him two."

Chapter Five

90. Acts 17:1-3, "Now when they had passed through Amphipolis and Apollonia, they came to Thessalonica, where there was a synagogue of the Jews. Then Paul, as his custom was, went in to them, and for three Sabbaths reasoned with them from the Scriptures, explaining and demonstrating that the Christ had to suffer and rise again from the dead, and *saying, 'This Jesus whom I preach to you is the Christ* (author's emphasis).'"

91. 2 Thess. 3:10, "We commanded you this: If anyone will not work, neither shall he eat."

92. 1 Thess. 2:9; 2 Thess. 3:7-8: "For you remember, brethren, our labor and toil; for laboring night and day, that we might not be a burden to any of you…For you yourselves know how you ought to follow us, for we were not disorderly among you; nor did we eat anyone's bread free of charge, but worked with labor and toil night and day, that we might not be a burden to any of you."

93. Acts 17:4, "And some of them were persuaded; and a great multitude of the devout Greeks, and not a few of the leading women, joined Paul and Silas."

94. See Acts 17:5-9.

95. Acts 17:10, "Then the brethren immediately sent Paul and Silas away by night to Berea. When they arrived, they went into the synagogue of the Jews."

96. Acts 17:11-12, "These were more fair-minded than those in Thessalonica, in that they received the word with all readiness, and searched the Scriptures daily to find out whether these things were so. Therefore many of them believed, and also not a few of the Greeks, prominent women as well as men."

97. Acts 17:13, "But when the Jews from Thessalonica learned that the word of God was preached by Paul at Berea, they came there also and stirred up the crowds."

98. Acts 17:14-15, "Then immediately the brethren sent Paul away, to go to the sea; but both Silas and Timothy remained there. So those who conducted Paul brought him to Athens; and receiving a command for Silas and Timothy to come to him with all speed, they departed."

99. Acts 17:11, "These were more fair-minded than those in Thessalonica, in that they received the word with all readiness, and searched the Scriptures daily to find out whether these things were so."

100. Acts 17:1, "Now when they had passed through Amphipolis and Apollonia, they came to Thessalonica, where there was a synagogue of the Jews."

101. 1 Thess. 3:1-2, "Therefore, when we could no longer endure it, we thought it good to be left in Athens alone, and sent Timothy, our brother and minister of God, and our fellow laborer in the gospel of Christ, to establish you and encourage you concerning your faith."

102. See James 3:13-17.

103. Jer. 17:5, "Thus says the Lord: 'Cursed is the man who trusts in man and makes flesh his strength, whose heart departs from the Lord.'"

104. Luke 24:49, "Tarry in the city of Jerusalem until you are endued with power from on high."

105. Acts 1:8, "You shall receive power when the Holy Spirit has come upon you."

106. 2 Cor. 3:5-6, "Not that we are sufficient of ourselves to think of anything as being from ourselves, but our sufficiency is from God, who also made us sufficient as ministers of the new covenant, not of the letter but of the Spirit; for the letter kills, but the Spirit gives life."

107. Phil. 4:13, "I can do all things through Christ who strengthens me."

108. 2 Cor. 12:8-10, "Concerning this thing I pleaded with the Lord three times that it might depart from me. And He said to me, 'My grace is sufficient for you, for My strength is made perfect in weakness.' Therefore most gladly I will rather boast in my infirmities, that the power of Christ may rest upon me. Therefore I take pleasure in infirmities, in reproaches, in needs, in persecutions, in distresses, for Christ's sake. For when I am weak, then I am strong."

109. Eph. 1:19-20, "And what is the exceeding greatness of His power toward us who believe, according to the working of His mighty power which He worked in Christ when He raised Him from the dead and seated Him at His right hand in the heavenly places."

110. John 15:4-5, "Abide in Me, and I in you. As the branch cannot bear fruit of itself, unless it abides in the vine, neither can you, unless you abide in Me. I am the vine, you are the branches. He who abides in Me, and I in him, bears much fruit; for without Me you can do nothing."

111. 1 Thess. 5:17, "Pray without ceasing."

Chapter Six

112. Acts 18:5-6, "When Silas and Timothy had come from Macedonia, Paul was compelled by the Spirit, and testified to the Jews that Jesus is the Christ. But when they opposed him and blasphemed, he shook his garments and said to them, 'Your blood be upon your own heads; I am clean. From now on I will go to the Gentiles.'"

113. Acts 18:7, "And he departed from there and entered the house of a certain man named Justus, one who worshiped God, whose house was next door to the synagogue."

114. Acts 18:8, "Then Crispus, the ruler of the synagogue, believed on the Lord with all his household. And many of the Corinthians, hearing, believed and were baptized."

115. Acts 18:8, "Then Crispus, the ruler of the synagogue, believed on the Lord with all his household. And many of the Corinthians, hearing, believed and were baptized."

116. Genesis 3:15, "And I will put enmity between you and the woman, and between your seed and her Seed; He shall bruise your head, and you shall bruise His heal."

117. Acts 18:18, "So Paul still remained a good while. Then he took leave of the brethren and sailed for Syria, and Priscilla and Aquila were with him."

118. Acts 18:21, "But took leave of them, saying, 'I must by all means keep this coming feast in Jerusalem; but *I will return again to you, God willing.*' And he sailed from Ephesus (author's emphasis)."

119. Jonah 8:3, "But Jonah arose to flee to Tarshish from the presence of the LORD. He went down to Joppa, and found a ship going to Tarshish; so he paid the fare, and went down into it, to go with them to Tarshish from the presence of the LORD."

120. Acts 18:23, "After he had spent some time there, he departed and went over the region of Galatia and Phrygia in order, strengthening all the disciples."

121. 2 Cor. 5:1, "For we know that if our earthly house, this tent, is destroyed, we have a building from God, a house not made with hands, eternal in the heavens."

122. Mark 6:3, "Is this not the carpenter, the Son of Mary, and brother of James, Joses, Judas, and Simon?"

123. John 14:1-2, "Let not your heart be troubled; you believe in God, believe also in Me. In My Father's house are many mansions; if it were not so, I would have told you. I go to prepare a place for you."

124. Matt. 8:11, "Many will come from east and west, and sit down with Abraham, Isaac, and Jacob in the kingdom of heaven."

125. Matt.17:3-4, "And behold, Moses and Elijah appeared to them, talking with Him. Then Peter answered and said to Jesus, 'Lord, it is good for us to be here; if You wish, let us make here three tabernacles: one for You, one for Moses, and one for Elijah.'"

PART TWO

Chapter Seven

126. Acts 19:35, ESV, "And who is there who does not know that the city of the Ephesians is temple keeper of the great Artemis, and of *the sacred stone that fell from the sky* (author's emphasis)?'"

127. 1 Cor. 16:19, "The churches of Asia greet you. Aquila and Priscilla greet you heartily in the Lord, with *the church that is in their house* (author's emphasis)."

128. Acts 18:24-26, "Now a certain Jew named Apollos, born at Alexandria, an eloquent man *and* mighty in the Scriptures, came to Ephesus. This man had been instructed in the way of the Lord; and being fervent in spirit, he spoke and taught accurately the things of the Lord, though he knew only the baptism of John. So he began to speak boldly in the synagogue. When Aquila and Priscilla heard him, *they took him aside and explained to him the way of God more accurately* (author's emphasis)."

129. Acts 19:9, "But when some were hardened and did not believe, but spoke evil of the Way before the multitude, he departed from them and withdrew the disciples, reasoning daily in the school of Tyrannus."

130. Gen. 4:22, "And as for Zillah, she also bore Tubal-Cain, an instructor of every craftsman in bronze and iron."

131. See Acts 19:13-16.

132. See Acts 19.

133. 1 Cor. 12:13, "For by one Spirit we were all baptized into one body—whether Jews or Greeks, whether slaves or free—and have all been made to drink into one Spirit."

134. Rom. 6:3-4, "Or do you not know that as many of us as were baptized into Christ Jesus were baptized into His death? Therefore we were buried with Him through baptism into death, that just as Christ was raised from the dead by the glory of the Father, even so we also should walk in newness of life."

135. Eph. 2:4-6, "But God, who is rich in mercy, because of His great love with which He loved us, even when we were dead in trespasses, made us alive together with Christ (by grace you have been saved), and raised us up together, and made us sit together in the heavenly places in Christ Jesus."

136. Eph. 1:3, "Blessed be the God and Father of our Lord Jesus Christ, who has blessed us with every spiritual blessing in the heavenly places in Christ."

137. 1 Peter 3:22, "[Jesus Christ] has gone into heaven and is at the right hand of God, angels and authorities and powers having been made subject to Him."

138. Eph. 1:22, "And He put all things under His feet, and gave Him to be head over all things to the church."

139. Isa. 40:31, "But those who wait on the Lord shall renew their strength; they shall mount up with wings like eagles, they shall run and not be weary, they shall walk and not faint."

140. Heb. 1:3-4, "[Jesus] being the brightness of His glory and the express image of His person, and upholding all things by the word of His power, when He had by Himself purged our sins, sat down at the right hand of the Majesty on

high, having become *so much better than the angels*, as He has by inheritance obtained a more excellent name than they (author's emphasis)."

141. See Isa. 14:12-15.

142. Eph. 6:12, "For we do not wrestle against flesh and blood, but against principalities, against powers, against the rulers of the darkness of this age, against spiritual hosts of wickedness in the heavenly places."

143. Eph. 6:11, "Put on the whole armor of God, that you may be able to *stand* against the wiles of the devil (author's emphasis)."

144. Mark 9:29, "So He said to them, 'This kind can come out by nothing but prayer and fasting.'"

145. Mark 16:17, "And these signs will follow those who believe: In My name they will cast out demons."

146. Jude 1:9, "Yet Michael the archangel, in contending with the devil, when he disputed about the body of Moses, dared not bring against him a reviling accusation, but said, 'The Lord rebuke you!'"

147. 1 Cor. 10:20, "Rather, that the things which the Gentiles sacrifice they sacrifice to demons and not to God, and I do not want you to have fellowship with demons."

Chapter Eight

148. Acts 19:10, "And this continued for two years, so that all who dwelt in Asia heard the word of the Lord Jesus, both Jews and Greeks."

149. Rom. 15:23, "But now *no longer having a place in these parts*, and having a great desire these many years to come to you (author's emphasis)."

150. Acts 20:16, "For Paul had decided to sail past Ephesus, so that he would not have to spend time in Asia; for he was hurrying to be at Jerusalem, if possible, on the Day of Pentecost."

151. Acts 19:21, "When these things were accomplished, Paul purposed in the Spirit, when he had passed through Macedonia and Achaia, to go to Jerusalem, saying, 'After I have been there, I must also see Rome.'"

152. Acts 20:17, "From Miletus he sent to Ephesus and called for the elders of the church."

153. See Acts 20:18-35.

154. Acts 20:22-23, "And see, now I go bound in the spirit to Jerusalem, not knowing the things that will happen to me there, except that *the Holy Spirit testifies in every city, saying that chains and tribulations await me* (author's emphasis)."

155. Acts 6:5, "And they chose Stephen, a man full of faith and the Holy Spirit, *and Philip*, Prochorus, Nicanor, Timon, Parmenas, and Nicolas, a proselyte from Antioch (author's emphasis)."

156. See Acts 8:4-8.

157. See Acts 8:26-40.

158. Acts 21:8-9, "On the next day we who were Paul's companions departed and came to Caesarea, and entered the house of Philip the evangelist, who was one of the seven, and stayed with him. Now this man had four virgin daughters who prophesied."

159. See Acts 10.

160. Acts 21:11, "Thus says the Holy Spirit, 'So shall the Jews at Jerusalem bind the man who owns this belt, and deliver him into the hands of the Gentiles.'"

161. Acts 21:13, "Then Paul answered, 'What do you mean by weeping and breaking my heart? For I am ready not only to be bound, but also to die at Jerusalem for the name of the Lord Jesus.'"

162. Acts 21:12, "Now when we heard these things, both we and those from that place pleaded with him not to go up to Jerusalem.

163. Acts 21:14, "So when he would not be persuaded, we ceased, saying, 'The will of the Lord be done.'"

164. Rom. 6:4-5, "Therefore we were buried with Him through baptism into death, that just as Christ was raised from the dead by the glory of the Father, even so we also should walk in newness of life. For if we have been united together in the likeness of His death, certainly we also shall be in the likeness of His resurrection."

165. Gal. 2:20, "I have been crucified with Christ; it is no longer I who live, but Christ lives in me; and the life which I now live in the flesh I live by faith in the Son of God, who loved me and gave Himself for me."

166. Rom. 6:3, "Or do you not know that as many of us as were baptized into Christ Jesus were baptized into His death?"

167. Col. 2:20-21, "Therefore, if you died with Christ from the basic principles of the world, why, as though living in the world, do you subject yourselves to regulations—'Do not touch, do not taste, do not handle?'"

168. Gal. 6:14, "But God forbid that I should boast except in the cross of our Lord Jesus Christ, by whom the world has been crucified to me, and I to the world."

169. Phil. 3:20, "For our citizenship is in heaven, from which we also eagerly wait for the Savior, the Lord Jesus Christ."

170. Matt. 6:19, "Do not lay up for yourselves treasures on earth, where moth and rust destroy and where thieves break in and steal."

171. Luke 9:23, "If anyone desires to come after Me, let him deny himself, and take up his cross daily, and follow Me."

172. 1 John 5:4-5, "For whatever is born of God overcomes the world. And this is the victory that has overcome the world—our faith. Who is he who overcomes the world, but he who believes that Jesus is the Son of God?"

173. 1 John 2:15-17, "Do not love the world or the things in the world. If anyone loves the world, the love of the Father is not in him. For all that is in the world—the lust of the flesh, the lust of the eyes, and the pride of life—is not of the Father but is of the world. And *the world is passing away*, and the lust of it; but he who does the will of God abides forever (author's emphasis)."

174. 1 John 5:19, "The whole world lies under the sway of the wicked one."

175. Rom. 12:2, "Do not be conformed to this world."

176. Gal. 1:4, "[Jesus] gave Himself for our sins, that He might deliver us from this present evil age."

177. Isa. 26:3, "You will keep him in perfect peace, whose mind is stayed on You, because he trusts in You."

178. Acts 20:24, "But none of these things move me; *nor do I count my life dear to myself*, so that I may finish my race with joy, and the ministry which I received from the Lord Jesus, to testify to the gospel of the grace of God (author's emphasis)."

Chapter Nine

179. Acts 9:15-16, "But the Lord said to [Ananias], 'Go, for he is a chosen vessel of Mine to *bear My name before* Gentiles, *kings*, and the children of Israel. For I will show him how many things he must suffer for My name's sake (author's emphasis).'"

180. Acts 24:10; 25:23-24: "The *governor* had nodded to him to speak…The next day, when Agrippa and Bernice had come with great pomp, and had entered the auditorium with the *commanders* and the *prominent men of the city*, at Festus' command Paul was brought in.²⁴ And Festus said: "*King Agrippa* and all the men who are here present with us, you see this man (author's emphasis)."

181. See Acts 25:1-12.

182. Acts 27:1, "When it was decided that we should sail to Italy, they delivered Paul and some other prisoners to one named Julius, a centurion of the Augustan Regiment."

183. Acts 27:3, "Julius treated Paul kindly and gave him liberty to go to his friends and receive care."

184. Acts 27:9, "Sailing was now dangerous because the Fast was already over." This Fast refers to the Day of Atonement in late September or early October.

185. Acts 27:13-14, "When the south wind blew softly, supposing that they had obtained their desire, putting out to sea, they sailed close by Crete. But not long after, a tempestuous head wind arose, called Euroclydon."

186. Acts 27:33, "Today is the fourteenth day you have waited and continued without food, and eaten nothing."

187. Acts 23:11, "The Lord stood by him and said, 'Be of good cheer, Paul; for as you have testified for Me in Jerusalem, so *you must also bear witness at Rome* (author's emphasis).'"

188. Acts 27:41, "But striking a place where two seas met, they ran the ship aground; and the prow stuck fast and remained immovable, but the stern was being broken up by the violence of the waves."

189. Acts 27:43-44, "The centurion ... commanded that those who could swim should jump overboard first and get to land, and the rest, some on boards and some on parts of the ship. And so it was that they all escaped safely to land."

190. Acts 28:1, "When they had escaped, they then found out that the island was called Malta."

191. See Acts 28:2-6.

192. Acts 28:10, "They also honored us in many ways; and when we departed, they provided such things as were necessary."

193. See Acts 28:12-15.

194. Acts 28:16, "When we came to Rome, the centurion...permitted [Paul] to dwell by himself with the soldier who guarded him."

195. Acts 28:23, 30: "*Many came to him* at his lodging, to whom he explained and solemnly testified of the kingdom of God, persuading them concerning Jesus from both the Law of Moses and the Prophets, from morning till evening... Then Paul dwelt two whole years in his own rented house, and *received all who came to him* (author's emphasis)."

196. Col. 1:7-8, "As you also learned from Epaphras, our dear fellow servant, who is a faithful minister of Christ on your behalf, who also declared to us your love in the Spirit."

197. Col. 4:12, "*Epaphras, who is one of you,* a bondservant of Christ, greets you, always laboring fervently for you in prayers, that you may stand perfect and complete in all the will of God (author's emphasis)."

198. 2 Cor. 11:28; Col. 2:1: "Besides the other things, what comes upon me daily: my deep concern for all the churches...I want you to know what a great conflict I have for you and those in Laodicea, and for as many as have not seen my face in the flesh."

199. Gal. 1:8-9; 5:12; Phil. 3:2: "Let him be accursed ... I could wish that those who trouble you would even cut themselves off…Beware of dogs, beware of evil workers, beware of the mutilation!"

200. Judaizers were Christian Jews who, during the apostolic and early postapostolic periods, attempted to impose the Jewish way of life on Gentile Christians. The Greek verb, which literally means "to Judaize," is found only one time in the New Testament (Gal. 2:14). There it means "to live according to Jewish customs and traditions."

201. Gal. 3:11, "No one is justified by the law."

202. Gal. 3:10, ESV, "For all who rely on works of the law are under a curse; for it is written, 'Cursed be everyone who does not abide by all things written in the Book of the Law, and do them.'"

203. Matt. 7:22-23, "Many will say to Me in that day, 'Lord, Lord, have we not prophesied in Your name, cast out demons in Your name, and done many wonders in Your name?' And then I will declare to them, 'I never knew you; *depart from Me, you who practice lawlessness* (author's emphasis)!'"

204. Gen. 15:6, "And [Abram] believed in the LORD, and [God] accounted it to him for righteousness."

205. Gal. 3:17-18, "And this I say, that the law, which was *four hundred and thirty years later*, cannot annul the covenant that was confirmed before by God in Christ, that it should make the promise of no effect. For if the inheritance is of the law, it is no longer of promise; but God gave it to Abraham by promise (author's emphasis)."

206. Gal. 2:21, "I do not set aside the grace of God; for if righteousness comes through the law, then Christ died in vain."

207. See Acts 15:1-31.

208. Col. 2:23, "These things indeed have an appearance of wisdom in self-imposed religion, false humility, and neglect of the body, but *are of no value* against the indulgence of the flesh (author's emphasis)."

209. Col. 2:10, "You are complete in Him."

210. Rom. 1:17, "The righteousness of God is revealed from faith to faith."

211. Col. 2:6, "As you therefore have received Christ Jesus the Lord, so walk in Him."

212. See Gal. 3:2-5.

213. Hab. 2:4, "The just shall live by his faith."

214. Gal. 3:24, "The law was our tutor to bring us to Christ, that we might be justified by faith."

215. Rom. 7:7, "I would not have known sin except through the law. For I would not have known covetousness unless the law had said, 'You shall not covet.'"

216. Rom. 3:20, "By the law is the knowledge of sin."

217. Gal. 3:25, "But after faith has come, we are no longer under a tutor."

218. 1 Tim. 1:9, "The law is not made for a righteous person, but for the lawless and insubordinate, for the ungodly and for sinners, for the unholy and profane, for murderers of fathers and murderers of mothers, for manslayers."

219. See Rom.7:1-4, 6.

220. Col. 2:20-21, "If you died with Christ from the basic principles of the world, why, as though living in the world, do you subject yourselves to regulations— 'Do not touch, do not taste, do not handle?'"

221. Gal. 5:1, "Stand fast therefore in the liberty by which Christ has made us free, and do not be entangled again with a yoke of bondage."

222. See Phil. 3:4-9.

Chapter Ten

223. See Col.4:7-14; Rom. 16:5-15; Phil. 2:25.

224. Gal. 5:13, "For you, brethren, have been called to liberty; only do not use liberty as an opportunity for the flesh, but through love serve one another."

225. Rom. 6:6-7, "Our old man was crucified with [Jesus], that the body of sin might be done away with, that we should no longer be slaves of sin. For he who has died has been freed from sin."

226. Luke 9:23, "Then [Jesus] said to them all, 'If anyone desires to come after Me, let him deny himself, and *take up his cross daily*, and follow Me (author's emphasis).'"

227. Matt. 27:39-42, "Those who passed by blasphemed [Jesus], wagging their heads and saying, 'You who destroy the temple and build it in three days, save Yourself! If You are the Son of God, *come down from the cross*.' Likewise the chief priests also, mocking with the scribes and elders, said, 'He saved others; Himself He cannot save. If He is the King of Israel, let Him now *come down from the cross*, and we will believe Him (author's emphasis).'"

228. Gal. 2:20; 1 Cor. 15:31: "I have been crucified with Christ; it is no longer I who live, but Christ lives in me; and the life which I now live in the flesh I live by faith in the Son of God, who loved me and gave Himself for me...I die daily."

229. Gal. 5:17, "The flesh lusts against the Spirit, and the Spirit against the flesh; and these are contrary to one another, so that you do not do the things that you wish."

230. Gal. 5:25, ESV, "If we live by the Spirit, let us also *keep in step with the Spirit* (author's emphasis)."

231. See Phil. 2:19-23.

232. See Phil. 2:25-29; Col. 4:7-9.

233. Rom. 6:11, "Reckon yourselves to be dead indeed to sin, but alive to God in Christ Jesus our Lord."

234. Col. 3:5-8, "*Put to death your members* which are on the earth: fornication, uncleanness, passion, evil desire, and covetousness, which is idolatry. Because of these things the wrath of God is coming upon the sons of disobedience, in which you yourselves once walked when you lived in them. But now you yourselves are to *put off all these*: anger, wrath, malice, blasphemy, filthy language out of your mouth (author's emphasis)."

235. 2 Cor. 4:10-11, "Always carrying about in the body the dying of the Lord Jesus, that the life of Jesus also may be manifested in our body. For we who live are always delivered to death for Jesus' sake, that the life of Jesus also may be manifested in our mortal flesh."

Chapter Eleven

236. Acts 20:29-30, "I know this, that after my departure savage wolves will come in among you, not sparing the flock. Also from among yourselves men will rise up, speaking perverse things, to draw away the disciples after themselves."

237. See Rev. 2:1-4.

238. Rev. 2:14-15, "I have a few things against you, because you have there those who hold the doctrine of Balaam, who taught Balak to put a stumbling block before the children of Israel, to eat things sacrificed to idols, and to commit sexual immorality. Thus you also have those who hold the doctrine of the Nicolaitans, which thing I hate."

239. Jer. 17:9, "The heart is deceitful above all things, and desperately wicked."

240. Lev. 11:44, "You shall therefore consecrate yourselves, and you shall be holy; for I am holy."

241. Rom. 6:1-2, "Shall we continue in sin that grace may abound? Certainly not!"

242. Heb. 13:4, "Marriage is honorable among all, and the bed undefiled; but fornicators and adulterers God will judge."

243. Mark 10:6-9, "From the beginning of the creation, God made them male and female. For this reason a man shall leave his father and mother and be joined to his wife, and the two shall become one flesh; so then they are no longer two, but one flesh. Therefore what God has joined together, let not man separate."

244. See Rev. 2:12-15.

245. 1 Tim. 1:3, "As I urged you when I went into Macedonia—*remain in Ephesus* that you may charge some that they teach no other doctrine (author's emphasis)."

246. 1 Thess. 3:1-2; 1 Cor. 4:17; Acts 19:22.

247. 1 John 4:15, "Whoever confesses that Jesus is the Son of God, God abides in him, and he in God."

248. Eph. 2:13, "But now in Christ Jesus you who once were far off have been brought near by the blood of Christ."

249. Eph. 1:5, "Having predestined us to adoption as sons by Jesus Christ to Himself, according to the good pleasure of His will."

250. Rom. 8:15, "You did not receive the spirit of bondage again to fear, but you received the Spirit of adoption by whom we cry out, 'Abba, Father.'"

251. Gal. 4:7, "You are no longer a slave but a son, and if a son, then an heir of God through Christ."

252. Eph. 3:12; Heb. 4:16: "In [Christ] we have boldness and access with confidence through faith in Him…Let us therefore come boldly to the throne of grace, that we may obtain mercy and find grace to help in time of need."

253. Matt. 7:11, "If you then, being evil, know how to give good gifts to your children, how much more will your Father who is in heaven give good things to those who ask Him!"

254. Rom. 8:16-17, "The Spirit Himself bears witness with our spirit that we are children of God, and if children, then heirs—heirs of God and joint heirs with Christ."

255. 2 Cor. 8:9, "You know the grace of our Lord Jesus Christ, that though He was rich, yet for your sakes He became poor, that you through His poverty might become rich."

256. John 3:35; 16:15: "The Father loves the Son, and has given all things into His hand…All things that the Father has are Mine."

257. 1 Cor. 3:21, "All things are yours."

258. Eph. 1:11, "In [Christ] we have obtained an inheritance."

259. Eph. 1:3, "Blessed be the God and Father of our Lord Jesus Christ, who has blessed us with every spiritual blessing in the heavenly places in Christ."

260. Phil. 4:19, "My God shall supply all your need according to His riches in glory by Christ Jesus."

261. Col. 2:3, "In [Christ] are hidden all the treasures of wisdom and knowledge."

262. Ps. 121:2, "My help comes from the Lord, who made heaven and earth."

263. 1 Tim. 2:1-2, "I exhort first of all that supplications, prayers, intercessions, and giving of thanks be made for all men, for kings and all who are in authority."

264. 1 Tim. 2:8, "I desire therefore that the men pray everywhere, lifting up holy hands, without wrath and doubting."

265. John 16:24, "Until now you have asked nothing in My name. Ask, and you will receive, *that your joy may be full* (author's emphasis)."

Chapter Twelve

266. 2 Tim. 4:21, "Do your utmost to come before winter."

267. 2 Tim. 4:9, "Be diligent to come to me quickly."

268. 2 Tim. 4:12, "Tychicus I have sent to Ephesus."

269. 2 Tim. 4:21, "Do your utmost to come before winter."

270. 2 Tim. 4:13 "Bring the cloak that I left with Carpus at Troas when you come—and the books, especially the parchments."

271. 2 Tim. 4:11, "Get Mark and bring him with you, for he is useful to me for ministry."

272. Acts 12:25; 1 Peter 5:13: "Barnabas and Saul returned from Jerusalem when they had fulfilled their ministry, and they also took with them John whose surname was Mark…She who is in Babylon, elect together with you, greets you; and so does Mark my son."

273. 2 Tim. 4:11, "Luke is with me."

274. Jer. 38:6, ESV, "So they took Jeremiah and cast him into the cistern of Malchiah, the king's son, which was in the court of the guard, letting Jeremiah down by ropes. And there was no water in the cistern, but only mud, and Jeremiah sank in the mud."

275. 2 Tim. 1:16-17 "The Lord grant mercy to the household of Onesiphorus, for he often refreshed me, and was not ashamed of my chain; but when he arrived in Rome, he sought me out very zealously and found me."

276. 2 Tim. 4:16, "At my first defense no one stood with me, but all forsook me."

277. 2 Tim. 4:6, "For I am already being poured out as a drink offering, and the time of my departure is at hand." A drink offering referred to the offering of wine poured around the base of the altar during the Old Testament sacrifices (see Num. 15:1-12; 28:7; Phil. 2:17).

278. Phil. 2:19-20, "I trust in the Lord Jesus to send Timothy to you shortly, that I also may be encouraged when I know your state. For I have no one like-minded, who will sincerely care for your state."

279. Phil. 2:22, "As a son with his father he served with me in the gospel."

280. Col. 3:3, "Your life is hidden with Christ in God."

281. 2 Cor. 5:21; Eph. 1:4; Rom. 16:10: "That we might become the righteousness of God in Him…holy and without blame before Him in love…approved in Christ."

282. Prov. 28:13, "He who covers his sins will not prosper, but whoever confesses and forsakes them will have mercy."

283. 2 Cor. 5:8, "We are confident, yes, well pleased rather to be absent from the body and to be present with the Lord."

Chapter Thirteen

284. 2 Tim 3:12, "All who desire to live godly in Christ Jesus will suffer persecution."

285. Ps. 16:11, "In [God's] presence is fullness of joy."

286. Ps. 56:3, "Whenever I am afraid, I will trust in You."

287. Heb. 13:23, "Timothy has been set free."

288. Rev. 1:11, "Write in a book and send it to the seven churches which are in Asia: to Ephesus, to Smyrna, to Pergamos, to Thyatira, to Sardis, to Philadelphia, and to Laodicea."

289. 1 Cor. 16:19; Col. 4:15; Philem. 2: "Aquila and Priscilla greet you heartily in the Lord, with *the church that is in their house*...Greet the brethren who are in Laodicea, and Nymphas and *the church that is in his house*...And to *the church in [Philemon's] house* (author's emphasis)."

290. Matt. 28:19, "Go therefore and make disciples of all the nations."

MAPS

Map 1, Paul's First Missionary Journey

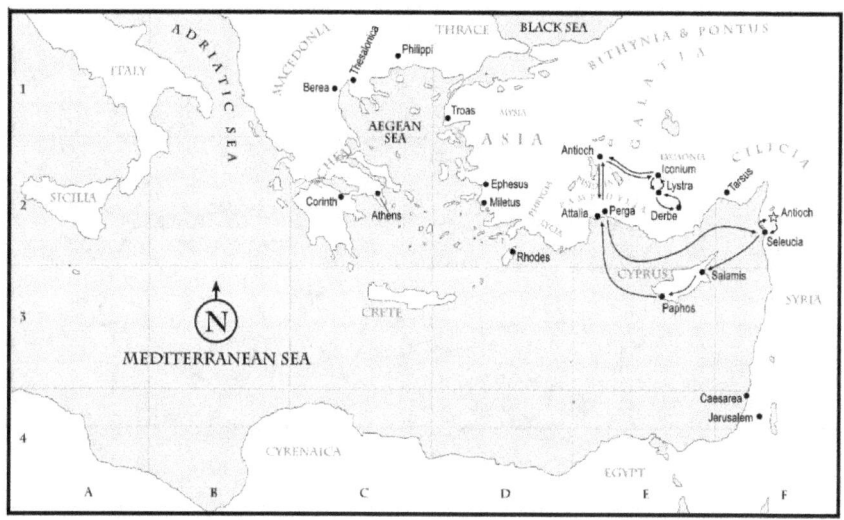

Map 2, Paul's Second Missionary Journey

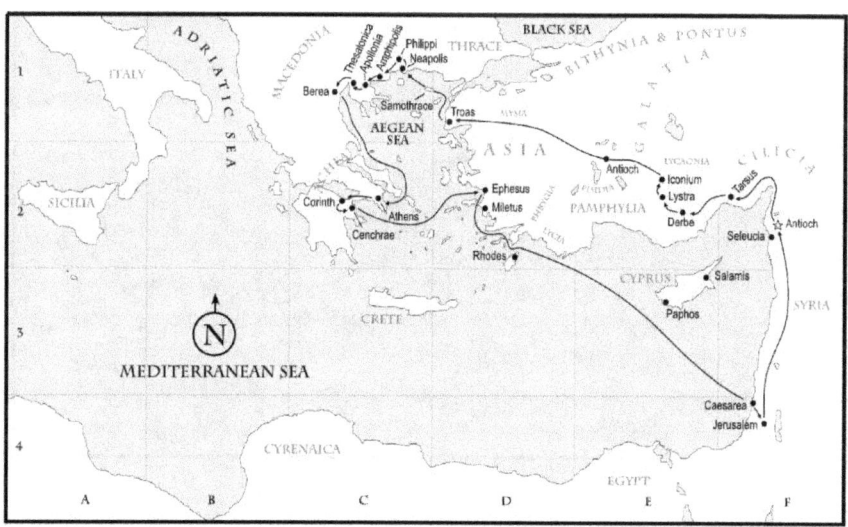

Map 3, Paul's Third Missionary Journey

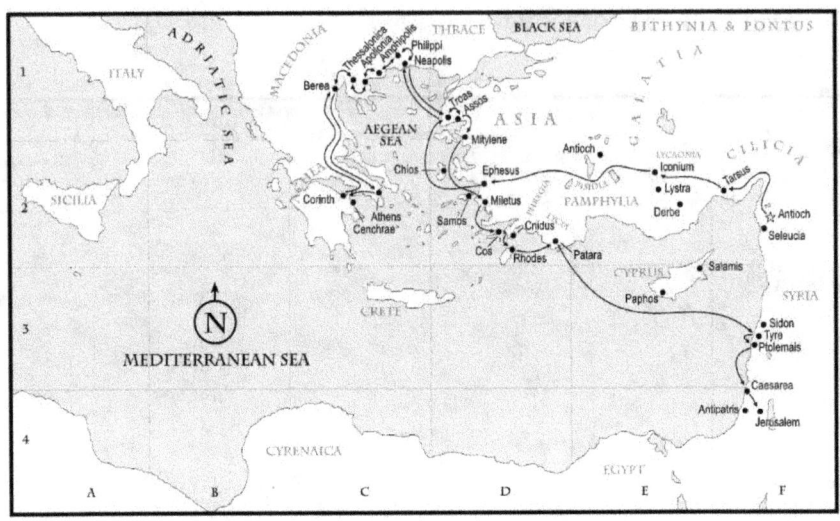

Map 4, Paul's Voyage to Rome

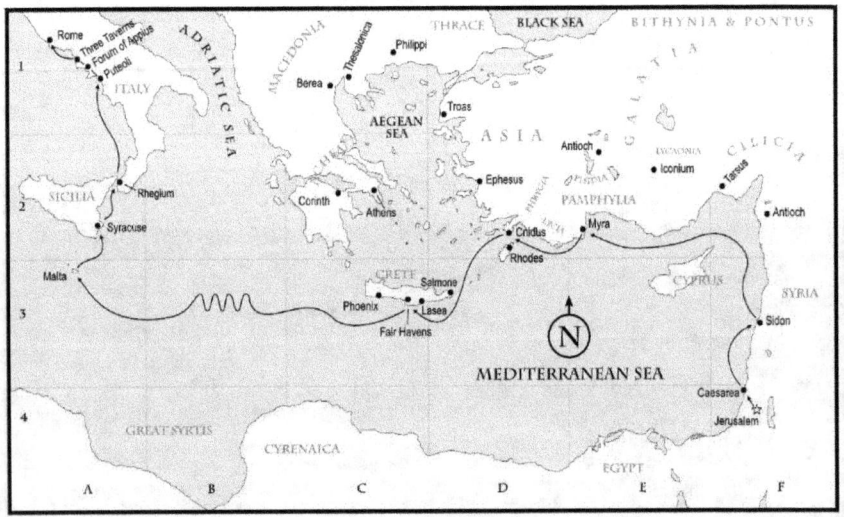

DR. MITCH MARTIN

Following in the footsteps of his ancestors, some of whom were circuit-riding preachers, Dr. Mitch Martin shares the gospel through story, symbol, and Scripture inclusion. Martin, a registered Chickasaw Indian from Oklahoma, is a graduate of Oklahoma Baptist University and Golden Gate Baptist Theological Seminary. He and his lovely wife, Myra, make their home in west Tennessee, where on a good day you can find him drinking coffee with a young champion talking about the ways of God. There's nothing Martin likes better than trying to make profound spiritual truths simple to grasp.

Please visit Mitch's website at:
www.MitchMartin.org